THE SWALLOW: A GHOST STORY

CHARIS COTTER

TUNDRA BOOKS

Published in Canada by Tundra Books,
a division of Random House of Canada Limited,
One Toronto Street, Suite 300, Toronto, Ontario M5C 2V6

Published in the United States by Tundra Books of Northern New York,
P.O. Box 1030, Plattsburgh, New York 12901

Library of Congress Control Number: 2014934478

LIBRARY AND ARCHIVES CANADA CATALOGUING IN PUBLICATION

Cotter, Charis, author
      The swallow / by Charis Cotter.

Issued in print and electronic formats.
ISBN 978-1-77049-591-3 (bound).—ISBN 978-1-77049-593-7
(epub)

      I. Title.

PS8605.O8846S83 2014   jC813'.6   C2013-906909-7
                                                 C2013-906910-0

Edited by Samantha Swenson
Designed by Leah Springate
Cover image © 2014 Kelly Louise Judd
Interior swallow image © kvasay / Depositphotos.com
The text was set in Sabon
www.tundrabooks.com

Printed and bound in the United States of America

1 2 3 4 5 6   19 18 17 16 15 14

PART ONE

THE HAUNTED ATTIC

There was no wind, and yet the air
Seemed suddenly astir;
There were no forms, and yet all space
Seemed thronged with growing hosts.
They came from Where and from Nowhere.
Like phantoms as they were.
They came from many a land and place—
The ghosts, the ghosts, the ghosts.

ELLA WHEELER WILCOX, "THE GHOSTS"

MISFIT

Polly

There's no place for me. I'm getting squeezed out of my own house. My parents want to save the world, and they're doing it one unwanted kid at a time.

The baby is the final straw. It was bad enough to have foster kids in and out of here every few months, and then it was even worse when Moo and Goo (the silliest teenagers you ever saw) came to live with us on a permanent basis. But at least I always had my own room.

I didn't want the baby and I told Mum that, but, as usual, she didn't pay any attention.

"It's up to us to give Susie a good home," she said in that social-worker voice of hers. "Not everyone is as lucky as you are, Polly. You need to learn to share."

Fine. Share my room. Share my clothes. Share my parents. Share everything until there's nothing left for me.

I know that's not Christian of me. My dad's a United Church minister, and over the years I've put in enough hours at church and Sunday school to know what it takes to be a good Christian. But I'm tired of sharing!

My room was the only place I had to myself in this crowded house. I had a desk by the window, looking out over the cemetery, where I used to sit and watch for ghosts as it got dark. I had a little bookcase and a big old chair for reading my ghost books. I loved my room.

But when Susie came, they put her crib in front of the window, and out goes my reading chair, and my desk gets shoved into a corner. They say there's nowhere else to put her. Lucy has her own room, because she needs to study all the time. Moo and Goo share a room, the Horrors share a room, and Mum and Dad sleep downstairs in what used to be the dining room.

Right from the beginning they said the baby would have to share with me. And right from the beginning I said I didn't want her. But I got her anyway.

The way I see it, my parents will keep packing kids into this house until we're stacked up in each room like sardines, and when there isn't an inch left they'll finally be happy and say, "Great, now we're taking care of all the kids in the world! No kids are sad or hungry, they're all here in our house." And then they'll forget which kids were theirs to begin with, and we'll all be one big happy family. Except for me.

Rose

I don't fit in. There's no place for me. Not at school, not with Mother and Father, not in this new house, not anywhere.

I don't belong here. My room looks like no one lives there, because Mother is so fussy about keeping things neat that I can't leave anything lying about, not even a book or a handkerchief.

I go for days without anyone speaking to me. The girls at my new school ignore me and so do the teachers. My parents are never home. That's why Kendrick is here, so they can stay out late working. After Granny McPherson died, we took over her house, and her ancient housekeeper came with it. Kendrick is slow, but she can still cook and do the housework. It doesn't take long because this house is like a museum—empty and quiet. She spends most of her time in her flat in the basement.

I don't even see Kendrick every day. Every night at 5:30 there is one place set at the dining room table. My dinner is on a plate with a cover to keep it warm, and a dish of dessert sits off to the side. I prop my book up against the silver candelabra to read while I try to force myself to eat.

Sometimes Kendrick shuffles into the living room while I'm practicing the piano and gives me a strange look. Sometimes I think she knows.

But she can't know. I keep it hidden from her, the same way I keep it hidden from Mother and Father and all my teachers and the girls at school.

I am bewitched.

HORRORS

Polly

All right, so maybe I'm exaggerating a little. The house won't hold ALL the unwanted children in the world. But we've already got seven kids and two grown-ups crammed in here, and it's not that big a house to start with.

It's in a row of old houses that are all joined together. It has high ceilings and funny little corners and big built-in closets. I've found some great hiding places, but the Horrors always seem to find me.

The Horrors are Mark and Matthew, my eight-year-old twin brothers. To get an idea of the supreme dreadfulness of the Horrors, imagine the worst brother in the world and then multiply by two—see what I mean?

They're nasty and annoying and determined to make me miserable. They follow me around singing, "Polly wants a cracker" and pretend I'm a parrot and make all these stupid bird jokes. They play tricks on me and go in my room and take my stuff, and they are always telling Mum if I do anything wrong. And because they are so cute, with their curly brown hair and blue eyes and freckles everywhere, grown-ups think they're full of mischief instead of full of evil.

I'm not cute. Not in the slightest. I'm too fat and I wear glasses. Mum says it's just puppy fat and it will disappear when I get to be a teenager and then I'll be just as pretty as Marian and Gudrun. I don't believe her. Anyway, those girls are so dumb. All they can talk about is boys, boys, boys. Marian, who's sixteen, sits around on the couch making cow eyes at her boyfriend, so I call her Moo. Gudrun, who's fifteen, slaps all this weird goo on her face to get rid of her pimples, so naturally I call her Goo.

I think I was pretty smart to think up their nicknames, but Mum said it was unkind. She wasn't even impressed with the way I made all my sisters' names rhyme: Lu and Moo and Goo—and now Sue, The Baby Who Stole My Room. Lu is the oldest (seventeen) and my real sister, just like Mark and Matthew are my real brothers. Mum says I shouldn't call them "real," but I'm determined to point out the difference, even if Mum and Dad aren't. I do realize that I'm stuck with Lu and the Horrors, because they're my family. What I don't see is why I should be stuck with the others.

I wish I were an only child.

Rose

You might think I'm exaggerating. That there's no such thing as being bewitched in 1963, in Toronto, Canada.

But that's how I feel. Like a princess in a story who has a bad fairy come to her christening in a cloud of black smoke. As if the

7

fairy pointed her wand at the lacy, innocent baby and said, "Winnifred Rose McPherson will go through her life seeing things that other people don't see. She will never be able to tell a single person about this because they will think she is insane."

Maybe you think that's not such a bad curse, like dying on your sixteenth birthday or spitting frogs whenever you speak. But let me tell you, some days I'd happily take the frogs or the poisoned spindle.

It all started when I was a baby. The things I see, the things that other people don't see? Ghosts. Ghosts everywhere.

When I was little, I didn't know they were ghosts. I thought they were people. It took me a long time to figure out that no one else could see them.

An old lady with a sad little smile used to come and sit in the corner of my nursery when I woke up crying in the middle of the night. My mother would bustle in, change my diaper and give me a bottle, while the old lady sat rocking back and forth, knitting. "There, there," the old lady would say softly. "There, there. Such a lovely baby. Such a good baby."

Mother never turned her head or paid any attention to her. But sometimes, when Mother was impatient with me, muttering, "Rose, Rose, why won't you sleep, Rose? I need my rest, I have to work in the morning. I'm so tired, won't you *please* just go back to sleep," the old lady had a strange effect on her. Gradually my mother would grow calmer, and soon she would fall into the same chorus: "There, there, such a lovely baby. Such a good baby." Rocked by their crooning, I'd fall asleep.

I didn't start talking till I was five years old. There was so much weird activity all around me, I thought the safest thing was to stay quiet and just watch. But my parents started bringing me to fancy doctors when I was two, trying to find out what was wrong.

Finally one morning at breakfast, I asked my mother to pass the marmalade. She dropped her teacup and my father nearly choked on his toast. Even the Breakfast Ghost jumped in alarm when he heard me speak. (He is an old man with thick white hair who sits beside me staring longingly at whatever I'm eating for breakfast.)

I'm still quiet. Unusually quiet, says my mother. Reserved, says my father. I'm trying to be very, very careful. If they find out I see ghosts, they'll think I'm crazy and lock me up.

I don't want that.

MIRROR

Polly

What I see when I look in the mirror:

Me. Polly Lacey, twelve years old. Boring brown hair that's too straight and just hangs there doing nothing. Glasses. Brown eyes. Chubby cheeks. Chubby all over. I don't think I'll ever slim down because I love food too much—chocolate especially.

I'm not exactly what you'd call a fashion plate. None of my clothes ever fit me properly; they're mostly hand-me-downs from my older sisters. And Mum says the reason I have to wear glasses is because I ruined my eyes reading in bed with my flashlight.

Favorite activity: Being alone, reading.

Favorite color: Red.

Favorite book: It's so hard to pick just one! I like ghost stories the best, and everything Philomena Faraday has written is fantastic! *The Silent Sorrowing Sadness* was the scariest, saddest book I ever read. But I also like mysteries—Agatha Christie, Nancy Drew—and kids' books like *Swallows and Amazons,* *The Hobbit,* all the Narnia books and all kinds of fairy tales, and Trixie Belden and—well, let's just say I love books.

Favorite place: The cemetery behind my house.
Secret desire: To see a ghost. A real ghost.

Rose
What I see when I look in the mirror:

Me. Winnifred Rose McPherson. My parents call me Rose. I am twelve years old, in Grade 7, and my birthday is December 5. I am a small person with a lot of black hair. It's thick and curly but it goes a little mad on damp days or when I brush it. Sometimes I fluff it around my face and look in the mirror to see if I could be at all pretty.

I'm not. I'm a sorry sight. I'm too pale and my cheeks are thin and I have big bags under my eyes because I don't sleep very well. My nose is a bit too big and crooked, and my mouth is a bit too thin. I'm small for my age. Mother says I need to eat more.

Favorite activity: I like singing. I like silence.
Favorite color: Purple.
Favorite book: *Jane Eyre* by Charlotte Brontë.
Favorite place: The attic.
Secret desire: To be normal and have a big, happy family.

INVISIBLE

Polly

I'm always trying to become invisible in this house, trying to find the one place I can be by myself where no one can bother me. It used to be my room. But since Susie made her appearance, I've been on the hunt for the perfect hiding place.

I thought I found one. Inside my closet, there's a built-in luggage loft. You go up a ladder and through an opening in the ceiling and then you're in a tiny room, just about three feet high. I moved the suitcases to make a wall so no one can see me if they look up from the closet, and then I made a little nest in the corner with some blankets.

I read my ghost books there and eat crackers and I feel safe. At least I felt safe until the Horrors started coming up after me. They think it's all a game of hide-and-seek, and sooner or later, they always find me.

They're not supposed to put even a foot inside my room, but they're always coming in anyway. When I complain to Mum she tells them off, but they keep coming back.

Now I don't know what to do. I have nowhere to go where

they can't find me. I just want one place that belongs to me and no one else. I want to be invisible.

Rose

Most of the time I feel invisible. I don't put my hand up at school anymore because the teachers never call on me. I drift through the halls past groups of girls talking and laughing, and no one even looks up as I go by.

It seems like the ghosts are the only ones who notice me. It's as if I have a big sign floating above my head saying: ATTENTION ALL GHOSTS!!! THIS ONE CAN SEE YOU!!!

It would surprise a lot of people in the world if they found out what ghosts are really like. Of course, some of them are scary—some are absolutely terrifying—and I've seen more than my share of those. But most of them are just dead people. Sad, lonely dead people. And once they realize I can see them they won't leave me alone.

It's the sadness that bothers me more than anything. Some are sweetly sad, like the old lady I saw when I was a baby. Others are miserably sad, and their unhappiness flows out of them like gray dishwater and floods over me. The angry sad ones are the worst. They're the dangerous ones.

GHOSTS

Polly

I've always wanted to see a ghost. More than anything. I keep watch at my window for hours, I go for walks in the cemetery almost every day after school and I read all the ghost books I can find at the Parliament Street Library.

It just seems to me that there's got to be more in this world than meets the eye. Ever since I was little I've wanted magic to be real. I want to see fairies and ghosts and witches riding their broomsticks across the sky. Life can't be as boring and ordinary as all the grown-ups make it out to be. There's just got to be more to it. I've always loved books where people stepped through doorways into other worlds, where horses had wings and children were swept away on marvelous adventures.

Of course, now that I'm older, I realize most of those things are not going to happen. But maybe I can still see a ghost! That's not impossible.

When I go to the cemetery I close my eyes and let the atmosphere just kind of soak into me. I start to tingle all over, and I think I hear whispering in the trees, and then I feel the presence of SOMETHING—but when I open my eyes there's nothing there. Just the gravestones, the trees and the road curving round the hillside.

It's disappointing. I've read that some people have the gift of second sight, and they live with one foot in this world and one foot in the next, so they can see what's going on with both the living and the dead. Sometimes they know when people are going to die.

I wish I had second sight. I want to see beyond this world. This world isn't all that wonderful.

Rose

I never want to see a ghost again. I'm sick of it. Ladies all in white who follow me down the street, sad men in suits who sit at the back of the bus, children in nightgowns floating out hospital windows—I wish they would all disappear.

When my father told me we were moving to Granny McPherson's house behind the cemetery, I was horrified. But what could I say? That living next to a cemetery wasn't a good idea for a person who could see ghosts? Not likely. I just kept quiet, as usual, and next thing I knew, we were here.

The first night in the new house I had a bad dream. I dreamed that all the ghosts from the cemetery were rising up out of their graves and drifting slowly towards the house. Over the stone wall at the end of the garden, up the garden path, passing silently through the bricks and the windows and the doors into my bedroom, crowding round my bed. Whispering.

All kinds of people in their grave clothes, all ages: babies, children, teenagers, mothers, fathers, old men and women—all sad, all lonely, all dead. They plucked at my blankets and my hair, and the murmur of their voices rose and fell like the sea. "Help me! Help me!" They kept coming until my room was full, and yet there were still hordes of them outside, crowding up against the window. I tried to sink down into the mattress to get away from them. My stomach turned over and over—and then I woke up. I was drenched in sweat and I felt sick.

The house was quiet. I turned on the light. There were no ghosts. But I didn't want to go to sleep again because I knew they would be waiting for me, just on the other side of the border between awake and asleep.

I picked up my book with shaking hands and began to read. It was book called *Jalna* that I had found on my grandmother's bookshelf.

I read for hours. Every time my eyes started to close I sat up and forced myself to stay awake and keep reading. When the light started seeping round the curtains I finished the book and then I finally let myself drift away. I slept without dreams until Kendrick woke me for breakfast.

The next night the dream came back. And the next night. I dreaded going to sleep. I read late into the night, trying to stay awake. It turned out that the *Jalna* book was part of a series about a big family, and my grandmother had them all, so I started to read my way through them.

Every night the pattern was the same. No matter how hard

I tried to stay awake, I still fell asleep eventually. Then the dream would come, with its crowds of clamoring ghosts, and I woke up in a sweat. Then I read until dawn, when I could safely fall asleep again.

We moved to the house behind the cemetery at the beginning of July. By the beginning of August, I was very, very sick.

HEADACHE

Polly

I woke up with a headache. Maybe that's why I lost my temper at breakfast.

It all began with eggs. Or the lack of eggs, to be precise. During the week we always have porridge for breakfast, but on Saturdays we get eggs. But this Saturday we had stupid old porridge again because Mum ran out of eggs on account of making deviled eggs on Thursday for some ladies from church who came over to have a meeting about "The Poor in our Midst" or something.

I was grumbling about the porridge and Dad took a deep breath and said, "Now, Polly," and I knew he was going to start off on another lecture about all the hungry children who would give anything to have lumpy old porridge day after day after day, so I jumped right in there.

"I don't care about those hungry kids so don't start telling me about them. All I care about is eggs. Saturday is eggs day and I want eggs!"

I picked up my bowl of porridge and slammed it down on the table, hard. The Horrors snapped to attention and nudged each other, staring at me and grinning. Moo and Goo rolled their eyes, and Lucy looked down her nose at me in disapproval.

"Polly, that's enough," said Mum automatically. "You're too old to be having temper tantrums at breakfast."

I knew she was right but that just made it worse. I picked up the bowl, higher this time, and dropped it again, really hard. It broke, and the gloopy porridge splattered all over the place.

Silence. Everyone held their breath. It was like that moment when a wave pulls back and another one is about to come roaring in.

Right on cue, Dad reared up.

"YOU!" he thundered, pointing a finger at me like he was the wrath of God and he was going to strike me dead with bolts of lightning. "YOU!! LEAVE THE TABLE THIS INSTANT!"

When Dad gets like that there is only one thing to do. Get out of the way, fast, or he'll start throwing things and yelling like mad. He's got a terrible temper, and Mum says I got mine from him, but he's bigger and way more scary than me, I can tell you. I think it's kind of hypocritical for a man of God to have such a vile temper, but if you think I'm going to tell him that you're crazy and you don't know my father.

I got out of there, fast, and went straight up to my hiding place in the loft. And there I stayed. After a while I ate some crackers and wished I'd eaten my porridge, because I was hungry. The house was really cold.

I cried a bit. I felt pretty bad. I knew I was being childish at breakfast, I knew I was being mean to my mum about the eggs, because she is really busy and can't always remember everything. But that just made me feel worse inside. And my head still hurt.

I was huddled up and miserable, like a wet bird with all its feathers fluffed up. I could hear the family carrying on as usual downstairs, just as if nothing had happened and I didn't exist. Just like normal. Finally I curled up and went to sleep.

Rose

My head was pounding. I had this weird floating feeling, like I was up above everything, looking down. Everything bleached out and turned white, and I couldn't tell who were the ghosts and who was alive.

The old lady came back and sat in the corner, knitting. I hadn't seen her since I was little.

The doctor had big bristly eyebrows and a huge mustache, and after a while he started looking just like a wolf, and he kept leaning over me and staring at me with his wild wolf eyes. I'm pretty sure I had been talking about the ghosts because I heard him say, "She's hallucinating."

Mother's face swam into view. She was crying. "My baby," she choked, "my baby."

"She'll be fine," said my father. He looked scared. Behind him the ghosts from the cemetery started streaming into the room, plucking at my sheets and my nightgown.

"GET AWAY FROM ME!" I screamed.

"We'll just get her to the hospital and see what we can do," said the Wolf Doctor.

"Such a lovely baby," said the knitting lady, rocking in her chair.

"My poor baby," said my mother, laying her cool hand on my hot forehead.

COLD

Polly

When I woke up it was even colder and really dark. I could hear the Horrors calling out to me. They were right inside my closet, at the bottom of the ladder.

"Polly wants a cracker, Polly wants a cracker," sang out Mark.

"We know you're up there, Polly-bird," sang out Matthew. "We're coming!"

"Matthew! Mark!" called my mother from downstairs.

They started to whisper.

"Come down here right now! I have a job for you," shouted Mum.

More whispering.

"Don't you worry, Polly-bird," said Matthew. "We'll be back!" They clattered off downstairs.

I had to do something. I just couldn't stand it anymore. I had to get away from them, somewhere they'd never find me.

In the ceiling of the loft there was a little trapdoor that led to the attic. Dad made me promise I'd never go up there because it wasn't safe. But I was so mad at him I didn't care about my promise. I heaved myself up against the trapdoor and pushed it open. I grabbed my book, a blanket and my flashlight, then hoisted myself into the attic and pulled the trapdoor shut.

The attic was cold and black as black could be. It smelled musty and forgotten. My flashlight cast a faint yellow light. I'd asked Mum for new batteries weeks ago but she was always forgetting stuff like that. I crawled into a corner by the wall and wrapped the blanket around me.

Dad had said the floor wasn't properly finished and would collapse if I walked on it. He said there were mice. But I didn't see any mouse poop and I didn't hear any scurrying. I didn't hear much of anything—no voices, no footsteps, no people. All the sounds of the house and the city were reduced to a faint murmur, far away, like the sea. It was very, very quiet.

As quiet as the grave, I thought, and then I sat up a little straighter. Maybe the attic was haunted! I closed my eyes to see if I could sense any ghostly presence.

But there was nothing there, just silence.

Rose

When I woke up in the hospital I was cold. I suppose I had kicked off my covers. I was shivering. There was no one there. No old lady, no mother, no father, no doctor. No ghosts. I pulled up the blankets and huddled under them, trying to get warm. I could see trees outside the window.

For a long time I drifted in and out of sleep, watching the leaves sparkle in the sunshine, happy to be alive, happy not to be haunted, even for a little while.

It did seem strange that I should feel so ghost-free in a hospital room. You would think hospitals would be full of ghosts. But when they finally let me go home, there were no ghosts there either. None. And no dreams. I still had that floaty feeling, as if I weren't quite there, and my head felt light. But I was well enough to start classes at my new school in the middle of September, and there were no ghosts there either. I didn't dare even hope that they were gone for good. Maybe some of the medicine they gave me in the hospital had driven them away for a while. For whatever reason, they were gone.

THE ATTIC

Polly

Hunkered down in my little nest, cozy under the blanket, I slowly started getting warmer. It was very restful to finally have a spot where no one could bother me, far away from sisters, brothers, parents and The Baby Who Stole My Room.

I found my place in *The Ghastly Ghost at My Gate* (the latest from Philomena Faraday) and began to read, holding the flashlight steady on the page.

> *Amanda stood frozen with fear on the pathway*
> *by the garden gate. The white figure floated closer*
> *and closer. It stretched out a bony hand and there*
> *was nothing she could do. She couldn't scream,*
> *she couldn't move, she could only stand, trans-*
> *fixed in terror as the hand reached towards her*
> *throat . . .*

A sudden breath of air ruffled the pages of my book. I gripped the flashlight firmly and swung it around the attic. The trapdoor was still shut tight. So where had the draft come from? And what was that smell that drifted in with it? Sweet, almost like candy, but sad too. A rose?

The attic was very still. My eyes drifted back to the page.

The wind howled around the shadowy garden. Amanda felt the cold touch of skeletal fingers on her neck, and then the wind whipped into a frenzy and the figure dissolved into a swirling white mist, wrapping around her like a shroud, and finally Amanda found her voice and screamed: a scream like a train hurtling round a corner at a hundred miles an hour, a scream that seemed to rise up from her toes and burst out the top of her head like a boiling kettle, a scream—

A floorboard creaked, very close by, and I was jolted out of the book and back into the attic. I held my breath and listened. Nothing. I shone the flashlight in a wide arc. The attic was still empty.

I drew a ragged breath. I was scaring myself to death with this ghost story. I settled back and found my place in the book again.

The fingers dropped from her throat and Amanda stumbled towards the house, but she tripped on a loose paving stone and fell. Immediately she was enveloped in a clammy mist, and she could feel

herself drowning in it, sinking fast. An icy voice
from beyond the grave whispered, "Beware!
Beware the ghostly gate!"

Right at that moment was when it happened. Someone—or some THING—started humming a tune, right in my ear!

I dropped the book and nearly dropped the flashlight. The light swung wildly. Trying to hold my shaking hands steady, I shone it around the attic. It was still empty, and the humming was getting louder.

I couldn't believing this was happening. I felt just like Amanda must have felt by the garden gate—unable to move or even squeak.

Then the humming turned into words, sung clearly in a sweet, high voice:

She's like the swallow that flies so high
She's like the river that never runs dry
She's like the sunshine on the lee shore
She lost her love so she'll love no more.

The tune was lilting and sad, like an old folk song. A girl was singing softly to herself, right beside me. But there was no one there. It had to be a ghost.

Rose

I finally found a place in this house that's my very own. I discovered it the week after I came back from the hospital.

I drifted into my grandmother's room one day, looking for the sewing basket so I could sew a button on my blue cardigan. Nothing had changed in there since she'd died in the spring.

Her bottle of Yardley's English Rose perfume stood on her dressing table. I untwisted the top and dabbed some on my wrists, then breathed it in. As the sweet, sad smell of roses flooded over me I wondered, for a moment, whether my grandmother would appear. She didn't. I thought I heard a sigh, but that was all.

Not seeing the sewing basket anywhere, I opened the closet door. I turned on the light, pushed some clothes to one side to search and then stopped. A ladder built flat against the wall led up to a trapdoor in the ceiling.

An attic. I hadn't even known the house had an attic, but when I pushed open the trapdoor and climbed in, it all seemed oddly familiar. The faded red-and-green cardboard boxes with "Christmas" written on the side, the ancient trunks shoved up against the wall, the discarded lamps, the broken chairs. Maybe I had come up here when I was little? I couldn't remember.

All that mattered was it felt safe. It felt like home. I started sneaking up there whenever I had the chance.

There was a stuffed chair in the corner and crates full of dusty old books. One box held what looked like every book L.M. Montgomery ever wrote. Another was full of ghost stories and books about ghosts.

I was especially interested in those. Over the years, I have quietly read everything I can about ghosts, trying to find something to help me ward them off. But I'd never seen books quite this old. Some of them were printed in the nineteenth century, with black leather covers and yellowing pages.

I brought up some cushions and a blanket to make a warm little nest in the chair. Then I stayed in the attic for hours, reading about ghosts by candlelight. I found it strangely comforting to sit in that silent, forgotten corner of the house, reading about other people besides me who saw ghosts. It made me feel that perhaps I wasn't completely crazy after all.

Sometimes I sang to myself. No one could hear me. At least, that's what I thought.

CONTACT

Polly

I felt a kind of pit opening up in my stomach like I was going to throw up. My body started tingling all over, like a really bad case of pins and needles.

"Who are you?" I croaked. But the singing went on, lilting and mournful.

> *'Twas down in the garden this fair maid did go*
> *A-plucking the beautiful—something rose.*

Then it stopped and a girl's voice said, "Darn it. What kind of rose? I can never remember what kind of rose."

Then the singing started again.

> *'Twas down in the garden this fair maid did go*
> *A-plucking the beautiful—blah blah rose.*

"Darn it," said the voice again.

I couldn't take it anymore.

"Who are you?" I said as loudly as possible.

The singing stopped. Silence.

"I know you're a ghost," I said, trying not to let my voice shake too much. "Stop trying to scare me and tell me who you are."

Silence. And then, finally, a cross little voice snapped at me out of the darkness.

"I'm not a ghost. Are you a ghost?"

I couldn't believe it. Here I was, talking to a ghost in my own attic!

"No, I'm not a ghost. *You're* a ghost. You're invisible."

The voice gasped. "I'm not! I can see my hands clearly. You're the ghost. You're invisible."

"I am not!" I replied. "I can see my hands too, but I can't see you. Where are you?"

"I'm in my attic," said the voice.

"I'm in MY attic," I said.

"I don't see you," said the voice.

"Well, I'm here, and I'd like to know why you're haunting my attic."

"I'd like to know why you're haunting MY attic," gasped the ghost.

This obviously wasn't getting us anywhere.

Rose

I felt sick to my stomach. I was not used to invisible ghosts. And I certainly was not used to ghosts that talked so much. Especially out loud.

My heart sank. I hadn't seen one ghost since I'd got home from the hospital, and I had really hoped they were gone forever. And now here was a ghost, right in my attic, in my own special nest. Where one came, the rest would follow, and I just knew I'd go stark raving mad if I couldn't keep them away from me.

"Tell me," said the ghost, "did you die a horrible death? Are you doomed to wander the ghostly regions between the land of the living and the life beyond?"

"Stop playing games," I said. "You know I'm not a ghost. You're the ghost, and you're pretending to think I'm a ghost to drive me crazy. It isn't going to work. Go away. All I want to do is sit in my attic and read my books and sing my songs in peace. Is that too much to ask?"

"Do ghosts read?" asked the ghost. "That's very interesting. Do you have to turn the pages or can you sort of absorb the story by holding the book and pulling the words into your head?"

"I—am—not—a—ghost!" I said slowly and firmly. "Ghosts don't read! They're ethereal. They haunt people. They follow them down the street, they watch them when they're doing their homework, they lurk behind gravestones, they hide in people's attics—"

"For someone who says they're not a ghost, you seem to know an awful lot about them," said the ghost.

I opened my mouth but no words came out. This was the most infuriating ghost I had ever met.

THE DISEMBODIED VOICE

Polly

It felt so good to have a chance to put my ghost lore to work.

"I can prove you're a ghost," I said. "I've just experienced four—no, five—classic signs of a ghostly presence. One—it's freezing cold—"

"We're in an attic!" said the ghost. "It's October! Of course it's cold."

"Two—I felt a draft but there was nowhere a draft could get in."

"We're in an ATTIC!" repeated the ghost. "Attics are drafty!"

"Three—I smelled an unusual smell, the smell of fresh roses, and there are no roses in this attic."

"My grandmother's perfume," said the ghost. "I put it on just before I came up here. I'm telling you, I'm not a ghost!"

"Four—I heard ghostly footsteps." The ghost tried to say something but I hurried on. "And five—I heard a disembodied voice singing a sad song."

"I am not a disembodied voice!" said the ghost. "I am a live girl, sitting in my attic, minding my own business until some crazy invisible ghost arrived and started tormenting me. You're not the first ghost I've ever met, you know! I'm not scared of you. Just leave me alone!"

"Look," I said. "It's okay. I understand. I've read all about this. Maybe you lived here long ago, and you died—and your spirit has been trapped in this attic ever since, and now I've been sent here to help you break free, and—"

There was a scrambling noise and then a THUMP! THUMP! on the wall behind me and the floor began to shake as if someone was stamping their feet.

"I—AM—NOT—A—GHOST!!" yelled the ghost. "MY NAME IS ROSE MCPHERSON AND I LIVE AT 43 CEMETERY LANE AND I AM TWELVE YEARS OLD AND I AM NOT DEAD!"

This ghost was angry.

Rose

It felt good to lose my temper. I made a lot of noise, but the ghost didn't seem at all put out.

"Wait. Where did you say you live?" she asked calmly.

"43 CEMETERY LANE!" I repeated.

Silence.

"Hit the wall again," suggested the ghost.

THUMP.

"Umm . . . Ghost?" she said.

"My name is Rose!"

"Ummm . . . Rose?" she said.

"What?"

"I live at 41 Cemetery Lane. Next door."

It took me a minute to figure it out. "You mean you're in your own attic? On the other side of this wall?"

"Yes," replied the ghost. "I guess you're not a ghost after all." She sounded disappointed.

"But why is it I can hear you so clearly?" I asked. "As if you were right here beside me?"

"I am right here beside you," she said, starting to tap against the wall. "This wall must be really thin, not like the brick walls downstairs."

"That must be it," I said. A great feeling of relief swept over me and I spoke without thinking. "So you're not a ghost either. You must be one of the dreadful Lacey children who live next door."

"Who says we're dreadful?" asked the girl.

Oops. "Um—my mother."

"Oh," said the girl. "Well—she's right. We are."

GHOST GIRL

Polly

My mind was ticking over pretty fast. If she really wasn't a ghost, how come I'd never seen her? How could a girl just my age live next door and me not know about it?

"Hang on . . . how come I've never seen you?" I asked.

"Not this again," said the ghost.

"It's a fair question," I said. "If you're not a ghost, and you really do live next door, don't you think I'd know?"

"Not necessarily," replied the ghost. "I'm an invisible kind of person."

wow. An invisible person. But not a ghost?

"What do you mean, invisible?"

"People don't notice me. I'm quiet."

"Quiet is one thing but invisible is something else. I think I'd be the first to know if a girl my age moved in next door."

The ghost sighed. "I haven't seen you either, but I've seen your brothers and several teenage girls, and your mother, who is always rushing in and out with a small child, and I saw your father when he had the fight with my father."

"Fight? What fight?"

"The day we moved in. Your father flew into a rage because our moving van was taking up all the parking space and he had to park on the next street."

"I never heard about that."

"My father thought your dad was going to hit him. He told me to keep away from your family, and my mother said you were all savages."

That got me worried. I was used to my dad losing his temper with us, but if he was starting to yell at the neighbors too, that was bad. I didn't know what was wrong with him.

"Yeah, well, I guess you have stayed away from us pretty good, since I've never seen you. When did you move in?"

"The beginning of July."

"I must have been away at camp. I never heard about new people moving in. What happened to the old lady who used to live there?"

"She was my grandmother and she died last spring."

"Oh. Sorry."

There was a silence. I still felt there was something fishy about her. She had an odd way of speaking, sort of old-fashioned.

"What school do you go to? Why don't I see you leaving in the morning?"

"St. Ursula's Academy. Private school. They start early. I leave at seven o'clock and I return by three."

"That explains it," I said slowly. "My bedroom's at the back—"

"So is mine," chimed in the ghost.

"I leave later than you do and I don't get home till about four."

"Satisfied?" said the ghost in a rather sarcastic tone.

"I guess so."

But there was definitely something weird about this girl. I wasn't really going to be satisfied until I saw her in the flesh and gave her a good pinch.

Rose

It was strange that I'd never seen her and she'd never seen me. Unless I really am invisible. Sometimes I wonder. Especially since I got back from the hospital. I feel so floaty and detached, and sometimes things start bleaching out and turning white again. But maybe that's because I've been calling on white light for protection, ever since I found that book in the attic.

It was called *Ghostly Phenomena*, written by a man named Roger Priestley. The last chapter was about protecting yourself from ghosts. One method is to use white light to keep them away. Apparently white light is pure, good energy that can block out bad spirits. The book provided instructions.

This is the way it works: I close my eyes and imagine white light washing over me and through me, and shining out around me like a suit of armor. It is so bright that it blocks out every little bit of darkness, so nothing is left but this shining, brilliant white.

I do this in the morning when I wake up, and at night before I go to sleep, and at odd times during the day. It makes me feel peaceful and safe. I think it might be helping to keep the ghosts away.

I have to say, I was relieved to discover that the Lacey girl was a living, breathing person and not a dead one. And she did know a lot about ghosts, which could be useful.

By a rather strange coincidence, I had run into her brothers the day before I heard her in the attic.

I'd come around the corner at the end of our block, walking fast, and bumped right into them. I dropped my schoolbooks.

"Pardon me," I mumbled.

I must have really startled them, because they jumped, yelled, and then stared at me in horror with their mouths hanging open and their eyes bulging. Then they recovered themselves and started in on me.

"Watch where you're going, why don't ya?" said one.

"Why are you sneaking up on us?" said the other. They both looked exactly the same, wearing matching blue zip-up jackets and brown pants. I found it a bit unnerving, as if I were seeing double.

"I apologized for bumping into you. Go away," I said, pushing past them.

"Yeah, well, YOU go away," said one, and "Keep your distance, Ghost Girl," shouted the other.

What could have scared them so much? I went home and looked at myself in the hall mirror. Ghost Girl?

Pale face, big dark eyes with hollows under them, dark gray school coat, hair all over the place. And a sad mouth.

I did look like a ghost.

PLAY DATE

Polly

"So, do you want to get together and play?" I asked the ghost. If she really was a ghost she'd make some excuse.

"I'm not allowed to play with you," replied the ghost in a tight little voice. "I told you, my mother thinks you're all savages, like your father. And your brothers, I might add."

"I won't argue with that, ghostie," I said cheerfully. "Your mother has the right idea. But we could meet in the cemetery and she'd never know."

"The cemetery?" said the ghost, her voice faltering. "Why the cemetery? Why not the park?"

"Because the cemetery is my favorite place. It's so spooky and mysterious, and it's deserted, and your mother would never run into us there."

"Well—"

"If you're really not a ghost, prove it. Come and meet me and show me that you're not dead."

Silence.

"I knew it!" I said. I couldn't help myself. "You ARE a ghost."

"Oh, very well," said the ghost. "I'll meet you tomorrow. By the big mausoleum with the angel on top. What's your name?"

"Polly," I replied. For someone who claimed not to be a ghost, she sure knew that cemetery pretty good. That mausoleum was way down at the bottom of the hill, and you couldn't see it until you were right up to it because it was built into the hill and there were lots of bushes around it.

"Polly. Fine. I'll see you there at two o'clock. I have to go to church in the morning."

"Me too. Then we have a big Sunday dinner, but I should be able to make it by two."

"Oh, and Polly?"

"Yes?"

"If you call me ghostie one more time you'll be really, really sorry. My name is Rose."

Rose

The really pathetic part of all this is that I did want to meet her. I never get asked to play by other girls. Never. Once in a while my mother sets something up with her society ladies who have children, but it never works. We sit staring at each other until the grown-ups finish talking. I never have a word to say.

I don't think I've ever really had a friend. I find it too hard to talk to people. Polly was different. Maybe it was easier to talk to her because I couldn't see her. And she was kind of funny, though annoying at the same time.

She certainly was dying to see a ghost. If only she'd known what seeing ghosts was really like, she would have run away from me as far and as fast as she could. Which is what she'd probably do anyway, once she met me and saw how weird I was.

CRYING

Polly

That night I woke up to the sound of my mother crying. It was very dark. She was lying beside me on my bed, the way she used to when I was little and had a bad dream. I rolled over and put my arm around her.

"Mum?" I whispered. "Mum, what's wrong?"

"Oh, Polly," she said. "I'm sorry about the eggs, I should have remembered." Then she hiccuped and started crying again and rocking back and forth.

"Never mind, Mum," I said softly. "It's okay. I'm sorry too."

And I was. I knew she meant well. She really does want to help all those children, because she has a good heart, but she gets too much to do and then she forgets about me. She always thinks I can manage, but sometimes I need her and she just isn't there. I wish it could always be like it was that night, with both of us sorry and both of us understanding what the other one needs, but I knew that the next day it would be business as usual, and Mum would be back to saying, "Polly, you have so much and so many children have so little and you need to learn to share," etcetera, etcetera.

But for the moment it was different. The house was very quiet. I could almost hear everyone breathing. Mum finally stopped crying. I think we both fell asleep, because I don't remember her leaving. But in the morning she was gone.

Rose

I woke up to the sound of my mother crying. It was very dark. I could hear her in her room, sobbing as if her heart would break. My father was away in Montreal on business, so she was all alone. Crying.

I got out of bed and walked to the doorway of her room.

"Mother?" I said, but my voice was swallowed up by the sadness in the room.

"My baby," she moaned. "My poor, poor baby. I've lost my baby."

I walked over to the bed. I hated to hear her cry. She was sitting up, her head in her hands. I touched her shoulder.

"Mother, don't," I whispered.

She looked up then, but I think she must have been crying in her sleep, because even though she was looking right at me, she didn't see me.

"I want my baby," she cried, "I want her back. Don't take my baby away."

Suddenly I caught a glimpse of something moving, something white, in the oval mirror above my mother's dressing table. I turned to look at it. Just then the moon must have come out from behind some clouds, because an eerie, cold light filled the room and I could see what was in the mirror.

It was me. I was wearing a white nightgown and my wild hair was tousled over my shoulders. My eyes were ringed with dark shadows. I seemed to float there, suspended in the glass.

I looked more like a ghost than ever.

GLOOM

Polly

It was the perfect day to meet a ghost in a cemetery. The gray sky felt heavy and foreboding. A chill wind sighed mournfully through the naked branches of the trees.

I shivered in the cold and stuck my hands deep into my pockets. I was wearing my red in-between coat and it wasn't really warm enough. The damp seeped through.

The cemetery was deserted. I shuffled through the drifts of crispy leaves past my favorite graves: Gower, Phyllis, age 8, 1853, with the fat little angel carved on the stone. Sharpe, Percy, age 12, 1906, guarded by two stone lions. Bakeapple, Victoria, age 2, 1873, with a wreath of stone flowers. Bakeapple, Anna, age 36, 1879. Victoria's mother, I guess. Their gravestones were blackened with age.

I had the feeling I always had in the cemetery: ghosts were all around me, but I couldn't quite reach them and I couldn't quite see them. Many of the gravestones were about my height, and when I turned my head quickly it looked like an army of people were filling up the hillsides behind me, watching me.

I could almost hear a murmuring of voices, I could almost see the dead children stretching out their arms to me, I could almost hear them whispering round my head—but there was no one there.

But maybe, finally, today would be the day.

I rounded the hillside and caught my first glimpse of the mausoleum. The angel loomed overhead, its enormous wings spread wide as if it wanted to block out the light.

Sure enough, someone was sitting on the steps below the barred gate to the tomb. A small, dark figure with a hood shadowing its pale face. As I drew closer, it raised its head to look at me.

A girl. A girl with a sharp little face, big dark eyes and a funny twisted mouth. She had shadows under her eyes, and she looked like . . . well, she looked like a ghost!

Rose

It was the gloomy, dark kind of afternoon that ghosts love best. When the whole world seems miserable, sad and empty.

I had come to the cemetery early, knowing how difficult it would be for me to go in. I stood outside the iron gates, trying to find the courage to walk through. I had said my white light prayers before I left home, but the weight of the ghosts beyond the gates pressed down on my chest so I could barely breathe.

The name of the cemetery, NECROPOLIS, was carved into the stone archway above my head. It meant "City of the Dead." People had been buried here for nearly two hundred years.

Famous rebels, writers, politicians, and ordinary people too: whole families, children, mothers and babies. Too many babies. Hundreds of ghosts, all clamoring for attention.

I peered in. The road lined with gravestones wound through tall old trees. There was no sign of the girl. There was no sign of anyone living.

I closed my eyes and tried to imagine the white light forming a suit of armor around me, a hard shell that would keep the ghosts out. My fingers and toes began to tingle with warmth.

I opened my eyes and walked through the gates. I moved quickly past the gravestones and down the hill to the mausoleum and sat on the steps, desperately muttering, "White light, white light" over and over again. I kept it up until a girl appeared in front of me, her eyes wide behind her tortoiseshell glasses. Her tight red coat stood out against the gray cemetery like a beacon of light.

THE GRAVESTONE

Polly

"Rose?" I asked in a high, squeaky voice.

The figure stood up and moved towards me. She was shorter than I was, wearing a long black cloak with a hood. She slowly stretched out her hand—JUST like Amanda's ghost in the book! I gasped and took a step backwards.

The girl stopped and rolled her eyes at me. Not in a ghostly way—more in a "I can't believe you're so dumb" way.

"I was just going to shake your hand," she said, her little mouth twisting in what could have been a smile. "To show you that I'm not a ghost."

Oh. I hesitated for a moment, watching her strange, big eyes, and then held out my hand. She gave it a sharp little squeeze and didn't let go. Her hand was very cold.

"Convinced?" she asked.

"I guess so," I answered, finally pulling my hand free.

"Oh no you're not," she snapped back at me. "You still think I'm a ghost. You think my hand is unnaturally cold and I'm weird-looking."

That was exactly what I was thinking. This girl was spooky.

"Let's walk," she said abruptly, looking over her shoulder and then hustling me down the road.

I looked back to see what she had been looking at. The angel hovered above us. Just underneath it the name of the family buried in the mausoleum stood out in large stone letters: MCPHERSON.

"What did you say your name was?" I asked her, trying to keep up. For a short person, she sure walked fast.

She flicked me a look and gave an impatient little shake of her head.

"Yes, that's my family's mausoleum," she said. "I'm Rose McPherson and there are three generations of McPhersons buried inside that hill."

I started to grin. "This is so exciting!" I said. "Tell me again you're not a ghost!"

Rose

"Rose?" said the girl in a squeaky, scared voice.

She was wearing a double-breasted red coat with six white buttons. It was too tight and the arms were a little short for her. Her tortoiseshell glasses turned up in little cat's-eye points that gave her a look of constant surprise. Straight brown hair and an eager puppy-dog expression. I could read her like a book. She really wanted me to be a ghost. She saw it as a game.

I wanted to get out of that cemetery as fast as possible. Outside my faltering circle of white light I could feel the ghosts straining to get through. The girl trotted along behind me, grinning like an idiot.

"Look," I said, "I'm not a ghost. But I do see them all the time. It's not fun."

"wow," she breathed. "You really see them? Do you see some now? Because I've got this really creepy feeling like they're all around us."

I walked faster. "Yes. They are."

Suddenly I felt a tug at my cloak, and I looked down to see a small child with a mass of blond curls, dressed in an old-fashioned white nightgown, looking up at me, pleading.

"Mama?" she said, her eyes brimming with tears. "Vicky wants her mama."

I shook her off impatiently and began to run. Polly came bumping along behind me, calling my name, but I skittered around the corner and headed towards the gates.

The fastest way to get out was to cut across an overgrown corner near the cemetery wall. The custodian hadn't bothered to cut the grass there for a while, and a few old gravestones rose up from a tangle of weeds. I leapt over a couple and dodged around a taller one, and then a crash behind me and a shout from Polly stopped me. I turned, gasping for breath. She had tripped on a gravestone and lay sprawled along the ground.

From the corner of my eye I saw movement, as white figures began to rise from the graves and seep towards me, just like in my dream.

"White light, white light, white light," I muttered desperately, stumbling back towards Polly. I had to get out of there.

I reached down to haul her up but she didn't move. She was staring at a gravestone, transfixed.

I looked at the stone. It read WINNIFRED ROSE MCPHERSON, 1910–1923.

DEAD

Polly

Everything went very quiet. A deep silence seemed to rise up from out of the ground around us. The ghost looked shocked. The color drained from her face and she began to sway.

Up until then I had been half-pretending. I don't think I really believed it. But when I lifted up my head after I fell, and her name was right there staring me in the face, I was convinced. She really was a ghost and she needed my help.

Rose

Suddenly it was silent. I could no longer hear the rustling of the wind in the trees and the hum of traffic on the expressway. My world shrank to those few words carved in stone: "WINNIFRED ROSE MCPHERSON, 1910–1923."

My name. Me? I felt like I was falling. I couldn't breathe. The gravestones and the trees started to spin, and then everything went black.

A string of pictures flickered through my brain, almost as if I were having a dream.

A bridge at night. The lights of the city, far away. A boy's face that looked very familiar. A screech of brakes and a thump—then a dizzying drop into nothingness, a fall that went on and on. A horrible thud.

"Rose? Rose? Are you okay?"

Polly's voice came from a long way off. Someone was pulling at my arm.

I opened my eyes. I could see the tracery of black tree branches against the gray sky. I was lying on something damp and hard. Polly was leaning over me and her fingers were digging into my arm.

"Rose?" she said again with a little squeak.

I focused on her rosy cheeks and the feel of her fingers through my coat. I took a deep breath. I could feel the cold air filling my lungs. Surely, surely if I were dead I wouldn't be able to feel that? And the damp leaves soaking through my stockings? And a stick poking into my leg?

I sat up. The gravestone was still there, with those words leaping out at me as if they were lit up in neon lights. WINNIFRED ROSE MCPHERSON.

What did it mean? I didn't feel dead. Not at all.

THE MYSTERY

Polly

"There's some mistake," said the ghost, scrambling to her feet and taking off again towards the cemetery gates. "I'm not a ghost."

I ran after her, watching my feet a little more carefully this time. She was out of the cemetery and off down the street by the time I caught up. "You do kind of look like a ghost," I panted. She was walking quickly now, casting glances over her shoulder every once in a while and muttering something to herself.

"And it's a bit of a strange coincidence, don't you think?" I went on. "Finding a grave with your exact name on it?"

Then she turned on me.

"I'm not . . . I'm not!" she said. "I'm alive. I'll prove it to you."

She was nearly crying. I felt so bad for her. Imagine, suddenly discovering that you're dead!

"How?" I asked.

"I don't know. But it has to be a mistake!" I repeated. "She could be a relative or from another branch of the family."

"What I wonder," said Polly thoughtfully, "is why aren't you buried in the mausoleum with all the other McPhersons? Why is your grave all by itself, shoved in a corner?"

I stared at her, remembering the brief vision I'd had before I fainted. The bridge. The fall. The thud.

"No," I said, shaking my head. "No!"

I started running again, but Polly grabbed my cloak and held me back.

"Rose," she said. "Just stop." Her face was full of concern.

"It's not true," I whispered.

"Maybe you're right. Maybe you're not dead. Let's find out, together. I'll help you."

For a moment I was tempted, but something in her eagerness made me suspicious. I broke free of her grasp.

"Leave me alone. You're still playing your stupid ghost game. If you only knew how horrible it really is to see ghosts, you wouldn't be so silly about it."

That's when she surprised me. Instead of snapping back at me her face lit up with a grin.

"I am silly, I know. I've just always had this thing about ghosts. But this is a real mystery, and it would be fun to find out what's going on. Don't you think?"

I stared at her. Fun?

"But what if it's true?" I croaked. "What if I really am a ghost?"

She put her arm through mine and started dragging me down the street.

"If you are, it's not so bad, is it?"

The wind was picking up now, whistling through the trees in the cemetery. The bare trees loomed over the street, forming an archway. Lights were coming on in houses and I could smell wood smoke from a fire. I felt the warmth from Polly's arm through my coat. She skipped a bit as she hurried me along, almost bouncing.

"No," I said slowly. "It's not so bad."

PROOF

Polly

At least I wasn't alone anymore. I liked Rose. I mean, maybe she was a ghost or maybe she wasn't, but either way, she was someone to talk to. She was kind of grouchy, but that didn't bother me. The great thing was that I was having a real adventure, just like a girl in a book.

Before we got home we decided on a plan of action. Rose was going to find out everything she could about the Mysterious Winnifred. Maybe she was a distant cousin or something like that. Privately, I still thought that Rose could be Winnifred, and she could have been haunting that house for years, thinking that she was alive and going to school and everything, but all the time she was really dead. I've read stories like that. And maybe the reason Rose could see all those ghosts was because she was one herself. But I didn't say that.

Anyway, we arranged to meet after school on Monday in the attic and talk about what she finds out. Meanwhile, my job was to try to find proof that Rose actually moved into that house last summer. Mum would know.

Rose

Despite everything, somehow I felt happier than I had for a while. It felt so good not to be alone anymore. Even if I was a ghost, at least I wasn't invisible to Polly, the way I was to everyone else.

Yikes! *Even if I was a ghost. . . !!!* The whole idea was preposterous. Polly was a nutcase, a very persuasive nutcase. But there were some weird things I couldn't explain. Why were Polly's brothers scared of me? Why was my mother crying in her sleep over losing me? Why was my name on a gravestone in the cemetery? Why did I feel so floaty, and drifty, and unconnected to the world, ever since I was sick in the summer? If you took everything into consideration, it looked pretty bad.

I didn't feel dead. But who knew what feeling dead was like?

As usual, no parents were around when I got home. Father wouldn't be back for a week or so, and Mother was out visiting. Even if they were home, how could I ask them if I was dead? It would be one more reason for them to think I was crazy and needed to be locked up. Or if I really was dead, what could they say? "Yes, dear, we wondered when you'd catch on. Now run along to heaven"? It was just too weird.

I told Polly I'd try to find out about Winnifred, so I went into my grandfather's study. In one of my searching-for-books expeditions I'd noticed a big old Bible on the bottom shelf. I knew that people used to keep birth and death records written in their family Bibles, so that seemed a good place to start.

The study was dim in the late-afternoon light. I quickly found the thick Bible and hauled it out. It was heavy, covered in cracked brown leather. The edges of the pages were tinged with gold that made a smooth, shiny surface when the book was closed.

I brought it over to the desk, switched on the lamp and opened it. Sure enough, there were names inscribed on the inside cover in different handwriting. Names and dates.

The first name was John Gerald McPherson, born 1806, Aberdeen, Scotland. He married someone named Margaret Campbell in 1829. They had seven children, and four died as infants. I ran my finger down the page. The first McPherson came to Canada in 1864, to Toronto, where he married Elizabeth Drummond. More marriages, births and deaths followed. My grandparents were there, married in 1909. And then that name, MY name, jumped out at me again, almost as suddenly as it had on the gravestone. "Winnifred Rose McPherson. B. Dec. 5, 1910, D. Jan. 8, 1923." Beside it was my father's name, "William George McPherson, B. Aug. 28, 1915. M. May 5, 1949, to Mary Louise McTavish."

My arrival on the scene, December 5, 1950, was not recorded. But this Winnifred person had the same birthday as me. And she'd died when she was around my age: thirteen.

DINNER

Polly

Dinnertime is always the same in my house. We eat squished around a table in the hallway, because we haven't had a dining room since the foster kids started coming in droves and crowding us all out. Eating in the front hall is ridiculous. Dad has to sit down first, because the dining table fills up the hall, and once he's in he can't get out without everyone getting up. He serves the meat from his end, then the plates get passed down to Mum to serve the vegetables. We all have to wait until everyone is served to start eating.

The Horrors make faces at me all through dinner. I try to ignore them, but every once in a while I lose it and start yelling at them.

Moo and Goo chatter on about school and boys and makeup and the latest rock-and-roll hits and all the other stuff they think is so very interesting, Lucy makes a few intellectual remarks about English lit or history that get Dad going off on some tangent, and Susie sits in her high chair and throws food around. I jump into the conversation wherever I can, although sometimes it just seems better to stay quiet and concentrate on eating. My family can make quite a racket over dinner.

Mum brought up my question for me. "Do the new neighbors have a child, Ned?" she asked as she nudged Mark's elbow off the table.

"I've never seen one," said Dad. "I find them quite stand-offish. I understand they used to live in Rosedale. Why they wanted to move down here is beyond me."

Rosedale is where the rich people live, on the other side of Bloor Street.

"There's always Ghost Girl," said Matthew, poking Mark in the ribs.

"Ghost Girl?" I asked. Nobody paid any attention to me.

"Don't be so foolish, Matthew," said Mum. "And don't talk with your mouth full."

Mark took over. "I've seen Ghost Girl floating in their front door. She dresses in black and she's really ugly and she talks to ghosts."

"I think she is a ghost," said Matthew. "She steals people's souls."

"What absolute nonsense," said Dad. "You're making it up. I've never seen any children there, just a woman and a man, leaving early and getting home late. Needless to say, I haven't spoken to them since that altercation when they moved in."

"You really were very unreasonable, Ned," said my mother with a sigh.

Moo and Goo started to giggle and Dad shot them a black look.

"Some people," he said gravely, "think they own the world."

Rose

Dinner was hot roast beef sandwiches with gravy, but I could barely eat a bite. I kept thinking about that page in the Bible.

When Kendrick came in to get my dishes, I blurted it out.

"Who was Winnifred Rose McPherson who died in 1923?"

Kendrick jumped. She wasn't used to me speaking.

"None of your business," she said.

"Who was she?" I persisted. "My aunt? Father's sister? Why have I never heard of her?"

Kendrick's mouth tightened in annoyance. She really didn't like me.

"If your father chooses not to speak of her, I don't think it's my place to."

I leapt to my feet, making her jump again.

"I have a right to know. Father isn't here. Tell me."

Kendrick stared at me. "You're just like her. That's the trouble." She picked up my nearly untouched supper plate and started towards the kitchen. I followed.

"How am I just like her?"

Kendrick shook her head. "I don't want to say. Ask your father."

There was a woman with gray hair in the corner of the

63

kitchen, ironing. She was dressed in a long, faded print dress that swept the floor, and she wore one of those old-fashioned aprons with a big bow at the back. She looked up at me with tired eyes and smiled a sad little smile, then went on with her ironing.

A ghost. They were getting into the house again.

"White light, white light, white light," I muttered.

Kendrick turned to see where I was looking. To her it was an empty corner of the room.

"Exactly like her!" she said bitterly. "She used to do that too. Seeing people who weren't there, talking to herself—crazy as a loon."

"How do you know I see people?" I asked her.

"I know the signs," replied Kendrick, plunging her arms into the dishwater. "I've seen it all before. That girl brought so much trouble to this house, it nearly killed her mother, and now here you are, another one, just the same."

"What trouble? What happened?" I asked.

Kendrick continued to wash the dishes. "I'm not saying any more. I've got work to do. You'd better get on with your piano practice, like your mother told you."

And that was that. There was no getting any more out of her.

THE DOOR JUMPER

Polly

I went right up to the attic after school the next day. I was half-afraid that Rose wouldn't be there, that she really was a ghost, or that I'd just imagined it all.

"Rose?" I said into the darkness.

No answer.

"Rose?" I said louder.

"I'm here," she replied. She sounded very far away.

"So? Did you find anything out?" I asked.

"Sort of," she said and then was quiet again.

"Well? What?"

"Winnifred was my aunt. My father's older sister."

"So how come you never heard of her? What did she die of?"

Silence.

"Rose! Rose, what's going on?"

"Look, Polly, it's just all really weird. Kendrick told me about her, she said that Winnifred was crazy and saw people who weren't there—"

"Ghosts," I breathed. "Just like you."

"Yes, apparently, just like me," said Rose softly. "She brought some kind of awful trouble to the house. That's all she would tell me."

"Sheesh."

"I found this Bible with our family names in it, and that's where I saw that Winnifred was my aunt, but the strange thing was—"

She stopped.

"The strange thing?" I urged.

"The strange thing was my name wasn't in it. I just wasn't there."

"You don't think—" I said breathlessly. "You don't think—"

Rose jumped in.

"No, Polly, I don't think it's because I'm really Winnifred's ghost! Why would Kendrick be talking to me if I were a ghost? Why would she be feeding me supper? Why would she talk about Winnifred as if she were a different person?"

"Well, maybe she's a ghost too, did you think of that? Maybe they're all ghosts, your mother, your father, maybe you're all trapped in this in-between world in that house where you all need to keep repeating the past over and over, and you—"

"Polly, get a hold of yourself," said Rose. "I'm not a ghost, all right? Get that out of your head! Something strange is going on but I—am—not—a—ghost!"

"My mother has never seen you," I said quickly. I couldn't help myself. "Neither has my father. My brothers have, but they think you're a ghost too. They call you Ghost Girl."

"Your brothers," retorted Rose, "are two nasty little boys who like playing tricks on people."

She had me there.

Rose

I was glad to get back into the attic. At least there were no ghosts there. Whatever had been keeping the ghosts away from me wasn't working anymore. The Breakfast Ghost had returned that morning, peering mournfully at my toast and marmalade. And another one had come the night before. A really scary one. But I wasn't going to tell Polly. She'd just start making up all kinds of theories about it and I couldn't take it.

What happened was, after supper I decided to look around in my grandmother's room to see if I could find out more about Winnifred. The door was closed. I turned the handle and took a step into the room.

Something black leaped out at me from behind the door. I put up my arm to ward it off. I felt a brief chill and a flash of hatred, and then it was gone.

It could have been a cat—except we don't have a cat. The room was empty. So was the hall behind me.

I moved slowly into the room, stepping carefully, keeping an eye out. Nothing. The hammering of my heart against my ribs started to slow down.

A ghost. But not the usual sort.

I began a search of my grandmother's room for some trace of my mysterious aunt. The bookshelves, the chest of drawers, under the bed. Nothing but dust there. Kendrick must not come in here very often.

I tackled the closet, still full of my grandmother's clothes. There were stacks of shoe boxes, so I dragged them out into the light and began to go through them.

My grandmother liked shoes. She had kept them in their original boxes.

Old-fashioned ones with laces, dress-up shoes with little bows, dancing shoes, sturdy oxfords, satin slippers. I tried on a pair of dark-red pumps that were only just a little loose. My grandmother had been tiny, like me. A full-length mirror stood beside the dresser, so I admired how the high heels made my legs look so grown-up all of a sudden. I shook out my hair and frowned at my reflection. My face was just too pale, and I had big bags under my eyes. There was a smudge on my nose. I took a step closer to see what it was—and suddenly my reflection whirled into darkness and the black thing was back, racing towards me out of the mirror.

I ducked. I felt the cold again, and the biting hatred, but nothing touched me. I opened my eyes.

It was gone.

SOCKS

Polly

"Ask your mother," I said. "She'll tell you about Winnifred."

Silence.

"Rose?" I asked. There seemed to be something wrong with her today.

"Ummm," came a murmur through the wall.

"ROSE!" I called. "What's going on?"

A big sigh. "It's not that easy," she finally replied. "You don't know my mother."

"What, is she mean or something?"

Another big sigh. Silence. I was just about to call out again when Rose spoke.

"No, she's not mean. She's just busy all the time. And I don't really . . . talk to her."

"Yeah, but you can ask her questions, can't you?"

"She would be very surprised if I spoke."

Silence again.

"I don't speak much. To anyone, really. Except you, now."

This was weirdness on top of weirdness. "You must speak.

I mean, don't you need to ask her for stuff? Like . . . um . . . clean socks?"

Rose gave a snort of laughter.

"Certainly not socks. Kendrick looks after the laundry."

I was searching through my mind for things I spoke to my mother about. "Don't you ever complain about stuff? Like maybe you don't like what's for supper, or you want a new sweater or something? Or you tell her what you did at school?"

"Not really. She's hardly ever here. She works all the time."

I was finding all this highly suspicious. I mean, every girl talks to her mother. Maybe her mother doesn't listen (like mine), but you gotta talk to your mother sometimes.

"Do you talk to your father?" I asked.

Impatient sigh. "No, not really. He's not here that much either."

"Where is he?"

"At work. Or traveling. He works for my grandfather's company, like my mother. He has to go to Ottawa a lot, and Montreal, and Windsor . . . and Vancouver sometimes. Lots of places."

"What kind of company is it?"

"Socks!" said Rose, snorting again.

"Socks?"

"Yes, socks. Haven't you ever heard of McTavish Socks?"

"McTavish Socks? You mean the ones that have that guy in the kilt and the mustache on every package?"

Another impatient sigh. "Yes, we're McTavish Socks. At least, my mother's family is, and she practically runs the company now because my grandfather is really old. My parents are always working. Sometimes I think they've forgotten they have a daughter because I never see them, and when I do we barely speak. They read the paper at breakfast, and the only person who notices me is the Breakfast Ghost and—"

"Breakfast Ghost?" I asked breathlessly. "Who's that? A real ghost?"

"Yes, I saw him today. He's an old man who wishes he could eat breakfast like he did when he was alive. He's been haunting me for years but he hasn't been around since we moved here. I guess he finally found his way to this house."

"Is he . . . is he . . . scary?" A ghost at breakfast! Would I ever like to see that!

"No, no, he's just an old man with a lot of white hair. I don't mind him so much. I just wish my parents would talk to me. How could I have an aunt I'd never heard about?"

How indeed, I thought. And how could she have parents who didn't see her or speak to her? Unless, of course, she was a ghost herself?

Rose

My parents have never talked to me very much. I don't know why. Maybe they got in the habit of not talking to me before I was five, when I didn't speak. When she does turn her attention my way, my mother always has a little frown on her forehead, as if I were another work problem that needs to be solved. For the past few months she's been more distant than ever. I've been worried about her. For some reason, she's sad. I can feel it. Her sadness is filling up this house.

Before Granny McPherson died, we lived with my McTavish grandparents in their big old house in Rosedale—I guess you'd call it a mansion, really. They're rich. My great-grandfather started the company a hundred years ago and it's the biggest sock company in Canada. My mother was the only child, so she was always going to inherit the business. It's unusual for a woman to be the head of a company like that, but she's really smart and she knows what she's doing. My grandfather trusts her. Father used to be a schoolteacher till he met Mother, and ever since then he's worked for McTavish Socks. When he is home, he's tired and distracted, like Mother.

She was sick for a while, last winter, and she went to the hospital for a couple of days. When she came back, she went to work as usual, but something was wrong. As usual, no one spoke to me about it. But I noticed she seemed sad all the time, and tired, and sometimes I heard her talking to my father late at night, and crying. One night I listened and I heard my father saying we needed to get away and live on our own, and be a real family. I guess that's why we moved here, to get away from my grandparents and be together.

But it hasn't worked out that way. They work more than ever. And I miss my room in the old house. It was on the third floor, with sloping ceilings, deep window seats and built-in bookshelves filled with my books and dolls and toys from when I was little. Above my bed was a beautiful painting of a mother with her baby.

We didn't bring anything here with us except our clothes. I don't feel like I really live here. I'm adrift in someone else's house. Compared to the big, airy rooms in our old house, this house feels small and dark and silent.

And now the ghosts are coming back.

SHOES

Polly

These long silences were getting spooky.

"Rose?" I finally asked. "Are you still there?"

"Yes," she said in a soft, faraway voice.

"Did you find out anything else last night?"

Rose laughed. "I did," she said in a louder voice that made her sound more like a girl and less like a ghost. "I went looking in my grandmother's closet to see if I could find any more traces of Winnifred. Apparently my grandmother loved shoes. There are piles and piles of shoe boxes in there. All different kinds of old-fashioned shoes."

"I'm coming over," I said, scrambling to my feet. "I gotta see them! I love shoes!"

"Wait a minute," sputtered Rose. "You can't just come over. I told you, I'm not allowed to play with you."

"Sneak me in," I replied. "What's the best door, front or back?"

I was going to see those shoes and nothing was going to stop me.

Rose

I'd never had a friend over to this house. I lived in silence. It seemed strange to bring someone in who was as lively as Polly.

As I edged down the stairs I could hear the sound of Kendrick's television drifting up from the basement. She wouldn't hear a thing.

I crossed the hall without making a sound and opened the front door.

PART TWO

THE HAUNTED HOUSE

Yet all things must die.
The stream will cease to flow;
The wind will cease to blow;
The clouds will cease to fleet;
The heart will cease to beat;
For all things must die.
All things must die.

ALFRED, LORD TENNYSON, "ALL THINGS WILL DIE"

ENTITY

Polly

I felt like I was in a horror movie. Where the girl goes slowly into the haunted house that's been deserted for years, step after step, and you want to tell her, "No, go back! Danger!" Rose's house had a hushed, still feeling—as though no one ever spoke out loud there.

Halfway up the stairs I started giggling, from being nervous, I think, and Rose looked really cross and told me to shush. The lights were low in the upstairs hall, and the corners were filled with shadows that flickered and grew as we passed by. All the doors were shut, and I had the uncomfortable feeling that there was something or someone behind them, listening to us.

The bedroom doors are never shut in my house, unless someone is getting dressed. Everyone always wants to know what everyone else is doing.

Rose led me into her grandmother's room. It was like stepping into an old picture. The four-poster bed stood shrouded in shadows and dark-red velvet curtains. My feet sank into the thick carpet, where bunches of pink and red roses twined together against a rich cream background.

"wow," I breathed. "This room is so spooky!"

Rose rolled her eyes. "Polly, you are so predictable."

"But it is!" I said. "Look at this place! And your whole house! It's like it's been preserved in time. I've always wanted to time-travel. Hey! What year is it, Rose?"

"It's 1963," she replied. "And I'm not a ghost. Can you just stop being so dramatic?"

"But why is this house so old-fashioned?" I persisted. "Didn't your parents bring anything new here?"

"No, they didn't. We only brought our clothes. Father wants to go through my grandmother's stuff and decide what to sell and what to keep. And my grandmother lived here for about sixty years, so of course it's old-fashioned."

"Okay, okay," I said, poking my head into the closet. "Where are the shoes?"

It happened without warning. Something black rushed at me from the depths of the closet and hurled me back into the room. I fell onto the thick carpet, knocking Rose over as I tumbled.

At first I thought it had to be a person who had been hiding in the closet. The twins love to jump out at me from behind doors to make me scream. Except this time there were no twins. There was nobody, just me and Rose.

Rose had gone white. She gripped my arms and stared wildly into my face.

"Polly, it wants to kill you!" she said.

Rose

The thing that knocked Polly over was bigger now. Bigger and darker. It passed through the room like a furious gust of hurricane wind. Now I knew what it was. And I knew what it wanted.

I had read about entities. Dark, fierce energies bent on evil. Whirlwind spirits that gathered up hate and despair, feeding on fear. They were very, very dangerous. Much worse than ordinary ghosts. The thing that struck me about them was their staying power. Some were hundreds of years old. They found a little pocket of hatred and festered there, lashing out when the living entered their domains.

I think I have encountered entities twice before the Door Jumper. Once, under a bridge in a ravine, I felt engulfed by a darkness that took my breath away and spun me around. I got away from there as fast as I could and never went back. Another time, passing an alleyway in the older part of downtown, I felt a stirring in the shadows at the foot of an ancient fire escape, and a trickle of malice sent an alarm through my body, like a tiny electric shock. I hurried along the street and left it behind.

The night before, I'd suspected the Door Jumper was an entity but I wasn't sure. This time there was no mistaking the gathering storm of rage. I felt its desire sweep over me like a wave of cold Atlantic water: it hated Polly. It wanted to obliterate her.

THE WINDOW SEAT

Polly

"Was that a ghost?" I whispered.

Rose suddenly cocked her head to one side, listening. Then she leaped up and started hauling me over to the bed.

"Quick, Kendrick is coming," she hissed, and I scrambled up onto the bed as she yanked the curtains closed.

The bedroom door crashed open.

"What's all this racket about?" barked a woman's voice. "You're not supposed to play in here!"

She didn't sound very nice. If that was the housekeeper, the only person Rose saw day in, day out—well, poor Rose!

"Mother doesn't mind," said Rose stiffly. "I'm not hurting anything."

"What I heard sounded like a herd of elephants charging about," said the woman. "What were you doing, jumping off the bed?"

"I tripped," said Rose coldly. "Now leave me alone."

Phew! I would never have talked to a grown-up like that!

There was a silence. I imagined them looking daggers at each other.

"This is your grandmother's room," said the woman in a different tone. She sounded sad now, sad and tired. "Your father wants it kept as it was. It's not a playroom."

"And I'm not playing," replied Rose.

Another silence.

"Supper in half an hour," snapped the woman, and the door closed behind her. We could hear her footsteps going down the stairs. Then Rose stuck her head through the curtains and grinned at me.

"All clear," she said.

I climbed down from the bed.

"You were wonderful!" I whispered. "She sounds like an old witch."

Rose nodded her head. "She is. She hates me. She worked for my grandmother for years, and I get the feeling she thinks we really don't belong here. But listen," she said, pulling me towards the window and talking softly, "we'll have to keep very still until she goes back to the basement. She'll be on the lookout now."

We settled into a window seat that had been obscured behind more heavy red curtains. It overlooked the cemetery. It was nearly dark, and the wind was high, chasing shadows up and down the line of gravestones.

I love the cemetery at that time of day. This view was almost the same as the one from my bedroom window. I could see the road winding down the hill, and the tall shapes of the monuments looming up, and the smaller gravestones huddling like a crowd of dwarves.

I looked over at Rose, about to tell her about the dwarves, but one look at her face stopped me. She was gazing at the cemetery too, but her expression was anything but peaceful. She looked sad—so sad—as if all the unhappiness of the buried dead were washing over her. But she also looked scared, as if she wanted to get up and run but she knew it would be no use.

I reached over and took her hand in mine and gave it a squeeze. Her eyes came back from the land of the dead and focused on me.

"You heard Kendrick. You heard her talking to me. So that proves I'm not a ghost."

"Not if Kendrick's a ghost too."

"Polly!" Rose pulled her hand away from mine. "Why can't you believe me? You must have seen Kendrick before. She's lived here forever. Are you telling me she was a ghost all that time?"

I shrugged. "Okay, I've seen her around. But not for a long time. I don't know, Rose. It's just all really . . . fishy. And mysterious. You've got to admit it's mysterious."

"Yes, but what you don't understand is that I've been living with ghosts all my life. I know what they're like, I see them every day. It's not a game to me. Can't you see how scary that Door Jumper is? Can't you see that if there was any chance—any chance at all—that I was really dead, that it would be the worst possible thing that could happen to me? I already feel invisible, I already feel like a total misfit, but if I were dead . . ."

She stopped and stared at me.

"There's nothing worse than being dead, Polly. Nothing."

She was right, of course. I felt really bad for getting her so worried. I reached out again and touched her arm.

"I'm sorry, Rose. I don't want you to be dead. I really don't. And I'm sorry I act like it's all a game. I can't help myself. It's my imagination. It always gets me in trouble. But now that I know ghosts are real, I think anything is possible, anything. And I want to solve the mystery, the Mystery of Rose, the Mystery of the Haunted House Next Door, the Mystery of the Ghost in the Closet—"

Rose started to laugh.

"That's exactly what I mean, Polly! You're talking like it's a book, like it's pretend, and it isn't!"

I smiled at her. "But isn't it more fun this way?"

Rose

It was almost too easy, sneaking Polly out. After Kendrick called me to supper she tramped downstairs to her basement lair, and Polly crept downstairs beside me and slipped out, mouthing, SEE YOU TOMORROW as I closed the door silently behind her.

Polly insisted she'd be coming back the next day to see the shoes. I knew if I could just figure out a way to keep Kendrick in the basement, we would be okay. To tell the truth, I was far more worried about the Door Jumper than Kendrick. I could handle Kendrick.

After supper I went upstairs and stood silently for a moment at the door of my grandmother's room. I was afraid to go in.

But it was just as we left it, with the curtains pulled back. The moon was rising up over the cemetery, and despite the fear that clutched my stomach I found myself walking to the window. The view was lovely in the moonlight. The shadows of the trees and gravestones were clearly etched now: black on silver, silver on black. It was almost peaceful. I leaned my face against the cold window.

That's when it came back. The Door Jumper. One minute I was alone, looking out at the cemetery, and the next I was enveloped in darkness and the moonlight snapped out as if someone had turned off a light.

It was different this time. I was in the center of a swirling blackness, as if someone had flung a huge black cloak around me, layers and layers of dark wool. But it didn't feel like it wanted to kill me. It was more like it was trying to tell me something, trying to get a message through.

"Winnifred?" I gasped. "Is it you?"

Instantly the entity changed. A roar like a freight train thundering through a tunnel filled my ears. Then I saw lights again and felt that falling sensation I'd had in the graveyard. Only this time there was no thud. I just kept falling and falling.

"STOP IT!" I screamed. "STOP TRYING TO SCARE ME!"

Then it was gone. I was kneeling on the floor by the window, and a shaft of moonlight lit up one of the big pink roses on the carpet in front of me.

COOKIES

Polly

I reached across Rose's bed for my sixth chocolate-chip cookie. Rose was still on her first, nibbling along the edge like a mouse. They'd been cooling on cookie racks when I came home from school, so I'd helped myself to a paper-bagful. Okay, so I was only allowed to take two at a time, but they smelled so good and I thought I should get a few for Rose. Who knew she could make one last half an hour? With any luck the twins would get blamed for the missing cookies and I'd avoid the "Polly, that's just greedy" lecture from Mum and the "Polly, you're getting fat" remarks from Moo and Goo.

"So, you really think the Door Jumper is Winnifred?" I asked through a mouthful of cookie.

Rose frowned. "You're getting cookie crumbs all over my bed, Polly. I'm not supposed to have food in my room."

"Sorry, sorry," I said, trying to brush them off and instead sending them flying all over the place. "But what about Winnifred? Why did you think it was her?"

"I don't know. I just got a very strong feeling. You know what I think, Polly? I think that room used to be Winnifred's bedroom. My grandparents probably slept in my parents' bedroom when Winnifred was alive. It's the biggest bedroom in the house and it has its own bathroom."

"You have two bathrooms? Wow," I said. "I thought our houses were the same, only backwards. We only have one bathroom. Sometimes I have to wait so long for Moo and Goo . . ." I stopped. Rose was frowning at me again.

"I guess the houses aren't identical," she said impatiently. "That's not the point. You see, if my grandmother's room was originally Winnifred's, then Winnifred could get up to the attic through her closet. And that's probably her stuff up there—the girls' books and the ghost books and the little reading corner and—"

"And she's still there," I breathed. "She's haunting your attic and her old bedroom!"

Rose

Polly's mother made good cookies. At least, they smelled delicious. But my stomach had been in knots since the night before and I could barely swallow.

I felt trapped. I didn't know how I was going to shield myself from this latest ghost. The white light didn't seem to be working. Not only was it an entity, the most dangerous kind of ghost, but it was also a relative. This haunting was personal. It wanted something from me. But all I wanted to do was crawl under my bed and stay there forever.

"You know what's really weird?" said Polly, reaching for yet another cookie. "That falling thing. You said you felt it before, in the cemetery?"

"Yes," I replied, brushing some more crumbs off the bed. "When we were at her gravestone. It was awful. I felt like . . . I felt like I was going to die."

Finally Polly stopped chewing. She just sat there staring at me.

"But you didn't? I mean, you were falling but you didn't hit the . . . the bottom?"

"I did in the cemetery. There was a sort of thud."

"Wow. A thud." Polly's eyes were very round.

"Yes, Polly, a thud. I hit the bottom. I died, okay? I'm dead, okay? That's what you want, right?"

"No, no, Rose, I don't," said Polly quickly, reaching out to me.

I closed my eyes and clenched my fists. "White light, white light, white light," I said over and over again.

"What?" said Polly. Her hand felt warm through my sweater. Warm and alive. I opened my eyes.

"I'm scared, Polly," I said faintly. "I'm really, really scared."

MUMBO-JUMBO

Polly

At that moment she looked more like a ghost than ever. Okay, okay, I know I said that before, but this time it was uncanny. Her face was white, except for the big black shadows under her eyes. She stared wildly at me and then started to sway back and forth, like she was going to keel over.

I took her by both arms and gave her a little shake.

"Rose!" I said urgently. "Pull yourself together! We're going to figure it out. We're going to go through it step-by-step and we're going to get all the evidence together and we're going to figure it out. I'll help, no matter what. I won't leave you."

Then she started to laugh, a kind of crazy, high-pitched laugh that sounded like it would turn into tears any second.

"You'll have to leave me if I'm dead, Polly. Unless I'm meant to just keep drifting around and haunting you and this house forever. I'll have to cross over, I'll have to go on to—to wherever, wherever they go, I don't know—"

"Rose!" I said, giving her another shake. "Maybe Winnifred can help us. Maybe if you help her she can help you. At least tell you whether or not you're a ghost."

"No, no!" said Rose frantically, "You don't understand. She's evil. She wants to kill you, Polly. She won't help. Ghosts don't help. They've never helped. All they want is to suck the life out of me and feed on it. They want to devour me. You can't ask them for help. They'll kill you."

"We can at least try," I said. "This one might be different."

Rose

Polly didn't have a clue. She had no idea what we were dealing with. But I had to calm down. Panic wasn't going to help. I closed my eyes and took a deep breath. I tried to picture the white light, spreading out from me, shining around Polly, protecting us, keeping us safe from the black anger of the Door Jumper and the steady clamoring of all the ghosts in the world.

It wasn't working very well. The light was trembling and shaky, exactly how I felt inside. I took another deep breath and started murmuring "White light" again. If only Polly hadn't half-convinced me that I was dead, I could have handled this. Like I always did. Somehow. Walked the line between the ghosts and the living, kept them at bay. But this time it was so much harder.

I opened my eyes.

"Have a cookie?" said Polly, holding the bag out to me.

To my surprise, I laughed. A real laugh this time, not a crazy one. Polly hesitated for a moment, then she grinned.

"What were you doing just now? Some kind of ghostie mumbo-jumbo?"

THE MISSING PHOTOGRAPHS

Polly

I'd never have told Rose this, but I really did wonder sometimes if she was a bit nuts. She was just SO WEIRD. When she shut her eyes and started chanting and taking really deep breaths I thought maybe she was finally going crazy. Driven mad by ghosts! The very thing she was afraid of.

Whatever she was doing, it did calm her down. And she said I could do it too, if the Door Jumper came back. I should just say it over and over again and imagine the white light.

"Like an angel?" I suggested. "Like a guardian angel, all white?"

She looked doubtful. Obviously she hadn't been to Sunday school as much as I had. But she said whatever worked for me.

The good thing was, the mumbo-jumbo made her feel better. She went downstairs to look for her grandmother's photo album while I lay back on her bed and watched the shadows flickering on the far wall. They were made by the tree branches outside her window, swaying up and down in the cold November wind. What I really wanted to do was get my hands on her grandmother's shoes, but a few more minutes wouldn't hurt. I closed my eyes.

I must have drifted off because it seemed like the next minute Rose was back, dumping a big heavy book on the bed.

"What did you find?" I said, sitting up. "Any pictures of Winnifred?"

"I don't think so," she said.

We opened the book together. It was a big, leather-covered album full of faded pictures of people in old-fashioned clothes: long summer dresses and fancy hairdos. The same people kept turning up: a little boy with a solemn expression, a man with thick curly hair, glasses, his mouth clamped firmly shut, and a small woman with a slight smile and eyes that looked out of focus.

"My grandmother," said Rose. "And my grandfather. And my father. But no Winnifred."

"Wait a minute," I said, turning a page. "Look at this."

Beside a picture of her father holding a bike that looked too big for him, I could see the faint outline of a square, half hidden behind the photograph.

"I think there was another picture here before," I said.

We both peered at the page. The outline was quite clear. It looked as though there had been two photos side by side, then one had been taken away and the other one pasted back in the center of the page. Flipping back and forth through the album, we found the same light indentations beside several pictures.

Rose looked at me. "You think they were pictures of Winnifred?"

"Who else?" I said.

Rose

"Why would they get rid of her pictures?" I asked Polly.

"Because she died?" said Polly, slowly turning the pages of the album. "Look, here's your dad when he was a teenager. He was cute!"

I looked over her shoulder. My father was definitely good-looking, with dark hair and eyes. But he wasn't smiling in any of the pictures. He looked sad.

I shut the album.

"Okay, she died. But why take her pictures away?"

"Maybe they couldn't bear to look at them," said Polly. "Maybe they were so filled with pain and anguish they didn't want to be reminded of her."

"Well, yes, that's a possibility. But it's almost as if she never existed. Except for the note in the Bible, there's no trace of her."

"Maybe Winnifred did something so terrible they wanted to pretend she never existed," said Polly, a faraway look in her eyes. "Maybe she murdered someone!"

"Polly! Stop being so dramatic! I don't think my aunt went around killing people."

Polly started counting on her fingers.

"Number one: you say the Door Jumper wants to kill me. Number two: you say the Door Jumper is Winnifred. Therefore Winnifred wants to kill me. If she succeeds, she will be a murderer. Maybe that's how she became an entity—because she was so evil. An evil murderer."

"Don't act like that makes any sense, Polly! You're just guessing."

"How do you explain it, then? How come nobody ever talks about her? How come there are no photographs of her?"

I couldn't.

ATTACK

Polly

Rose stuck her head out the door and listened.

"All clear," she breathed, and we tiptoed across the hall and into the Haunted Room.

In the late-afternoon light the room looked spooky but not terrifying.

"Shoes . . ." I whispered.

"All right, but I'm looking for clues too. There's got to be something in this room that will tell us more about Winnifred."

She went to the closet and pulled out the boxes. No sign of the Door Jumper.

The shoes were amazing. Perfectly preserved, all wrapped in tissue paper. Some looked as though they hadn't been worn.

"This is like Christmas," I said as I opened up box after box of exquisite footwear. "All I ever get new is plain oxfords for school. The rest are hand-me-downs." I touched the soft pink satin of a pair of pumps.

"Ooo, these are so soft," I murmured, holding one against my cheek and closing my eyes dreamily.

Rose rolled her eyes and laughed.

"They're just shoes, Polly!"

I don't know why, but I've always loved shoes. I beg Mum to buy them for me but, "There's no money in the budget to waste on shoes you don't need," she says. So I cut pictures of shoes out of magazines and draw outfits to go with them. If I were rich I'd have a closet full of shoes, just like Mrs. McPherson.

The next box contained black leather lace-ups, with pointy toes and two-inch heels. I tried them on. Just a little tight.

"My feet are bigger than yours and your grandma's," I said sadly.

Rose was admiring a pair of green suede slingbacks in the full-length mirror. They looked funny with her gray school uniform skirt.

"Did your grandma go to a lot of parties?" I asked, opening another box and reaching through the rustling tissue to pull out a pair of white satin dancing shoes with the cutest little pearl buttons you ever saw.

"I don't think so," said Rose distractedly. She had just dumped another four boxes on the floor. We had a lovely mess going, tissue paper and shoes littered all over the rose-covered carpet. Rose had turned on the lamp on the dressing table. It had a stained-glass shade of mauve and yellow and cast a soft glow.

"They must have had money, to buy all these shoes. What did your granddad do?"

"He was a doctor," said Rose, rummaging in the closet for more boxes. "I think he was kind of strict, from things my father has told me."

She plopped herself down on a scrap of empty carpet and opened another box. "My father said my grandmother never argued with him, always said, 'Yes, dear, you know best.' When my father finished university he wanted to be a journalist, but his father didn't like the idea and that was the end of that. He didn't think it was respectable, so my father went to teacher's college instead."

"But now he's not a teacher, he works at your mother's company, right?" I asked, running my finger along a smooth black velvet shoe.

"Yes," said Rose. "And he travels all the time. I miss him."

I looked at her. She looked sad again.

"I miss my dad too," I said suddenly. I'd never thought of it that way before, but it was true.

"But your dad is home every night," said Rose.

"Yes, but when I was little I spent more time with him, before Moo and Goo came, when the twins were younger. Mum would be busy with them, Lucy would be off doing her homework and Dad and I would have long talks in his study. I used to sit at a little table and pretend it was my desk, and he gave me paper and pens and I drew all these squiggly lines and pretended I was writing, just like he did. I used to be his special girl . . ." My voice faded away and I looked up, shocked at what I heard myself saying.

Rose was giving me an odd look.

"Baby stuff," I said, trying to laugh. "Silly baby stuff."

"What happened?" she asked quietly. "Why did it change?"

I felt the familiar anger rising up inside of me and I couldn't help myself.

"Moo and Goo happened," I said bitterly. "Apparently they're a lot more fun than I am. They're always bouncing around the place, giggling, whispering, teasing—my dad just switched over to them and forgot all about me."

My voice was shaking and I guess I was talking way too loud, because Rose suddenly said, "Sshhhh!" and cocked her head, listening. Then she jumped to her feet.

"Come on, let's go up to the attic," she said and bundled me into the closet.

I was halfway up the ladder when the Door Jumper returned. I felt the breath knocked out of me as surely as if someone had walloped me with a baseball bat. But this time it didn't knock me over. I clung to the rungs of the ladder and closed my eyes.

"BEGONE, FOUL BEAST!" roared Rose from behind me in a terrible voice. I could hardly believe it was hers, and I thought, Well, if old Kendrick didn't hear us before, she'll sure hear us now, and I scrambled up the rest of the way and heaved myself into the attic.

Rose didn't come up right away. As I lay huddled in a heap by the open trapdoor, I could hear her opening the bedroom door.

Something strange was happening to me. I felt sick, like I wanted to throw up, and the room started to spin. I lay down on my back and the floor rocked. Rose's white face appeared in the opening.

"Are you okay, Polly?" she asked, climbing up and sitting down beside me. She reached a hand out and touched my shoulder lightly. It was like the soft touch of a bird's wing.

Rose

There was something wrong with Polly. She wasn't getting up. The only light was filtering up from the bedroom through the trapdoor. I touched her shoulder.

She moved then, but it was small, the way a bird flutters when it's hurt and can't fly.

"Polly!" I said again, leaning in to look at her face. "What's wrong?"

"I don't know," she whispered. She looked frightened and very, very pale. "I feel sick."

I laid my hand on her forehead. It felt cold and clammy.

"Can you sit up?" I asked her.

She made that small flutter again, her legs and arms twitching.

"No," she breathed and shut her eyes.

I whirled over to the corner, turned on the light and grabbed the thick wool blanket from the chair to try to warm her up. She whimpered.

A feeling of dread was rising in my throat, making me sick. What had Winnifred done to her?

As soon as that thought entered my head I heard a high laugh from behind me. I spun around and for a moment I saw the figure of a girl, about my size, standing in the far corner of the attic, just outside the circle of light from the lamp. All I could see was her long hair, a dark dress with a wide white collar and two glittering eyes—and then she disappeared in a swirl of black shadow.

"What are you doing to her?" I cried out, striding towards it. "You're hurting my friend. Stop it at once!"

The blackness spun away as I approached, whirling over to the other side of the attic, where Polly was. I threw myself at it.

"LEAVE HER ALONE!" I screamed as it loomed over her.

And then the shadow blinked out and was gone. Just as it left I heard a girl's voice hiss in my ear, "Get her out of my attic!"

Polly lay perfectly still. She looked white as chalk. It might have been a trick of the light, but for a moment it seemed as if she was fading, and the outline of her figure grew dim among the shadows. I took her firmly by the arms and somehow, pushing and pulling, managed to get her down the ladder and into my grandmother's room. As soon as her feet touched the carpet she started to move again and mumble, and I got her over to the bed.

"I'll just get you some water," I said and tore out to the bathroom.

When I got back she was still lying back against the pillows, but she had a bit of color coming back into her face. I held the glass for her to sip.

"Rose," she said hoarsely, gripping my arm. "Rose, I thought I was dying."

OLD CLOTHES

Polly

The water tasted sweet and cool. It felt so good to be lying on Rose's grandmother's bed inside the dark red cocoon of the hanging curtains. They were partway open, showing the dim room beyond, illuminated by a kaleidoscope of colored light from the stained-glass lamp on the dresser. Rose covered me with a wool afghan from the window seat. She sat beside me on the bed, looking down at me with a worried frown.

"She wants you dead," said Rose finally. "But I don't know why."

I snuggled down more comfortably under the afghan. "I could feel the life draining out of me. It was so scary. I just felt weaker and weaker."

Rose looked over her shoulder at the open closet door. "She spoke to me, at the end. She said to get you out of her attic."

"Her attic?" I asked. "You think it is Winnifred, then?"

"Oh, yes," replied Rose grimly. "It's Winnifred all right. I saw her for a moment. In the corner. A girl my age with long hair and scary eyes."

"We've got to find out more about her," I said. "But what about Kendrick? Did she hear us?"

Rose shook her head. "No. I thought I heard something, but there was no sign of her. I guess she's decided to ignore me, no matter how much noise I make."

"How come you spoke in that terrible voice, 'Begone, foul beast!'?" I asked sleepily. "You sounded like an avenging angel."

Rose laughed. "I guess it does sound pretty strange. I read about it in a ghost book somewhere. It said that you're supposed to speak directly to ghosts and tell them to go away. And for demons and entities and stuff like that, you need to speak their language, like in the Bible. It's silly, really."

"Not silly," I mumbled. "Funny, though. And I think it worked. I think you scared her away."

"Let's hope so," said Rose, standing up. "I'm going to search this room. There's got to be something here that will tell us more about Winnifred."

She started with the closet, hesitating before stepping across the threshold. But it seemed safe, and she disappeared inside for a moment. She came out with more shoe boxes and then went back in again.

After five minutes of quick trips in and out, she had a collection of about fifteen more shoe boxes, two small suitcases and a couple of large cardboard boxes.

"There," she said, dusting off her hands. "Maybe there's something in all of this."

I sat up. "Can I—?" I started, but then I felt dizzy and lay back down.

Rose came and again laid her cool hand against my forehead.

"You're warmer now," she muttered, "but I'm a little worried about you, Polly. You should probably go to bed. Maybe I can take you home and we can tell your mother you're feeling sick?"

I shook my head. "No, I don't want her to know I've been here. I—I want to keep you to myself. Our secret."

Rose shook her head. "I don't know."

"I'll be okay. Just let me lie here for a while. Supper isn't till 6:30."

There was a funny little old-fashioned green alarm clock beside the bed, a round one with brass bells on top. It said 5:45.

Rose shook her head again, but then she plonked herself down among the shoe boxes and started going through them, throwing off the lids. I didn't get to see all the shoes this time. She moved quickly on to the suitcases.

"Wow!" she breathed as she opened the first one. She held up a pink filmy nightgown. It had thick borders of lace along the neck. Then she pulled out another one of creamy satin and another, dark-green silk. I was dying to get out of bed and look at them but she moved on to the other suitcase.

The fasteners were stuck at first and she had to bang them a bit to get them open. When she looked inside I could hear her quick intake of breath.

"What?" I asked eagerly, leaning out of the bed dangerously to try to see in.

Rose stood up and brought the case over to the bed.

Lying on top was a carefully folded black dress, and underneath were other dark sweaters and blouses, and a skirt. A pair of plain black shoes was tucked into the side pocket.

"So?" I said, puzzled. "Old clothes, so what?"

As Rose pulled out the dress, something dropped out of it and fell to the ground with a soft rustle. She picked it up. It was a dried flower—a rose—probably red once but now blackened with age. She handed it to me, then held up the dress. It was long. It would have probably hit Rose halfway between her knee and her ankle if she'd put it on. It had a row of buttons all the way down the front and a wide white collar.

I still didn't get it. "It's kind of hideous, but what's so special about it?"

"It's the same dress!" whispered Rose, fingering the soft material. "The one she was wearing when I saw her in the attic. I noticed the collar. These are Winnifred's clothes."

"Your grandmother kept them? After Winnifred died?"

Rose nodded.

I glanced down at the preserved rose in my lap. A faint, very faint, smell of roses wafted gently through the room.

Rose

The smell of roses. My grandmother's favorite perfume. Where was she? Why didn't I see her ghost? The room was full of her and yet—and yet—she wasn't quite there.

I reached into the suitcase and pulled out a black wool cardigan, then a dark silk blouse, some thick, itchy-looking stockings, a tweed skirt, the shoes. As I laid each item of clothing out on the bed, something in the room seemed to issue a soft sigh. And with the sigh came the faint smell of roses again. The clothes got smaller as I dug farther into the case: a baby's white ruffled christening gown lay at the bottom and a pair of knitted white baby socks.

Polly sucked in her breath when she saw the socks.

"Oh, Rose," she said softly. "This is the saddest suitcase."

I sank back beside her on the bed and contemplated the array of clothing. The bigger things were dark, but the smaller ones had some color: a small blue sweater had the sweetest little buttons in the shape of white sailboats.

"My grandmother must have packed this away and kept it all these years."

"All these years," echoed Polly, touching the socks. "It must have been so awful to lose her little girl. She must have missed her so much."

"Little girl? Don't you mean the murderer?" I couldn't help myself.

"Oh, all right. Maybe she wasn't a murderer. But even if she was some kind of criminal, her mother would still miss her, wouldn't she?" Polly's eyes were filling with tears. "That's what mothers do, don't they? Love their kids no matter what?"

I patted her shoulder. "Come on, Polly, let's get you home. You're upset. Are you strong enough to walk?"

She was. The house was very quiet. Polly passed silently through the hall and down the stairs behind me. No sign of Kendrick.

I slipped on my jacket and walked Polly to her door.

"Don't come in," she said. "I'm fine."

She didn't look fine. Her face was still pale and she looked shaky. Without thinking I reached out and gave her a big hug.

"Go to bed," I whispered. "Take care, and don't worry. We'll figure it out."

She smiled at me and went in.

I turned to go down the porch steps and stopped abruptly, almost falling. Her twin brothers stood on the front sidewalk, looking up at me, their mouths wide open.

I steadied myself against the railing and started down towards them. One of them stepped forward, his fists raised.

"What are you doing to our sister, Ghost Girl?" he demanded. He sounded fierce but his arms were trembling.

The other one stepped up and raised his fists in an echo of his brother.

"Leave her alone!" he sputtered. "Let her be!"

I stared at them. What was wrong with these kids?

"Your sister is my friend," I said finally. "I would never hurt her."

The first one let out a howl. "LIAR!" he shouted. "You are hurting her! You're trying to steal her soul! Go away!"

His brother grabbed his arm. "Be careful, Mark," he warned. "She might come after us too."

I gathered myself together and tried to tower over them. Since they were almost as tall as I was, this was challenging.

"Stop your nonsense," I said in a grown-up voice. "I am not a ghost! You're imagining things. Your sister is perfectly safe."

At this the second one—Matthew, I guess—began to cry. "No," he said. "No she isn't safe. She'll never be safe again."

I moved towards him, and then they both yelped and took off around the side of the house.

As I let myself in the front door, I thought, the Horror Twins were right. I didn't know how they knew, but I was putting Polly in danger, just by letting her into my house. I vowed that she would not come to visit again.

THE CRACK

Polly

I dreamed I was back in the attic. A full moon shone in through a skylight, and the shadows of gravestones marched along the sloping roof. There was a loud noise, like a thunderclap, and everything shook. An earthquake? I shut my eyes. When I opened them, a huge crack had appeared, running down the wall of the attic. As I gazed at it in horror, it slowly started to grow wider.

I reached for Rose but I couldn't find her. I could feel that same fading, draining feeling I'd had when the Door Jumper attacked me.

"Rose!" I called out, my voice a hoarse whisper. "Rose, help me!"

"Help you?" came a voice from the crack. I looked, and I saw Rose climbing through it with a strange look on her face. She was wearing the long black dress from the suitcase, the dried rose the color of old blood pinned to her chest. Her hair was longer, disappearing down her back in a swirl of shadows. "Can't you figure it out, you stupid girl?"

She stood over me and smirked. Her face was Rose's face, but it looked different: cruel and crazy.

"I am Winnifred," she said, leaning down and breathing into my face. "I am Rose. We are one. And you are dead."

With a howl of laughter she whirled around and snapped into the swirling, towering Door Jumper, surrounding me, hugging me, drowning me.

Rose

After supper I returned to my grandmother's room. I turned on the pretty stained-glass lamp and looked around at the mess. Tissue paper, shoes and boxes in a jumble on the floor. The sad clothes laid out on the bed. A few boxes were piled in a corner, still unopened.

I sat down in the middle of it all and started putting away the shoes, carefully wrapping them in the tissue again. It reminded me of when I was little, putting my dolls to bed. I had gone through a stage of dressing them all in makeshift nightgowns and setting them in cradles and shoe box beds, all in a row. Every night I had to do it, before I went to sleep. My mother would try to hurry me up but I had to make sure each one was carefully tucked in. Sometimes the old lady ghost would appear, rocking and knitting, smiling at us all: dolls, child, mother.

I don't know why, but there among the shoes and tissue I began to cry. I felt lost, as though someone had died and the world wasn't the place it was supposed to be.

"Never mind," came a familiar voice from the corner. "Never mind, dear."

I looked up. The old lady had appeared in the easy chair by the window, knitting. I hadn't seen her since the summer, when I was so ill.

"Who are you?" I whispered, getting up and drawing closer to her. "Why do you come to me?" I was at her feet now. She looked as solid as the chair she was sitting in. She was very old, shrunken and wrinkly, but her thick, arthritic fingers moved quickly in rhythm, and the needles clacked industriously.

"What are you knitting?" I asked, examining the soft, mauve wool that puddled on her lap.

She smiled at me. "It's for you, Rose," she said in her soft, sweet voice. "To keep you warm. You're going to need it."

I laid my head down against her knees then. I could feel her thin bones against my cheek, and she was strangely warm, for a ghost.

"Can you help me?" I asked. "Can you tell me what's going on?"

The knitting needles stopped clicking and she stretched out her hand and stroked my hair.

"Yes, I can help you, Rose," she said softly. "I'm watching over you. Always. You'll figure it out soon. Don't worry."

Then she was gone and I was leaning against an empty chair.

BEFORE BREAKFAST

Polly

Somebody was sitting on my stomach. Somebody else was sitting on my legs. I tried to kick them off but they just rearranged themselves and settled on top of me again. I opened my eyes.

"We need to talk to you, Polly," said Mark.

My bedside light had been switched on. Mark and Matthew were perched on top of me, wearing their matching Superman pajamas. Susie was sitting up in her crib, thumb in her mouth, staring at them. It was still pretty dark outside. The house was quiet.

"Okay, what?" I mumbled, trying to sit up and failing. They had me pinned to the bed.

"Don't try to get away," said Matthew. "This is serious."

"What do you want?" I said a little more clearly. This was no way to wake up, especially after a bad dream.

"First of all," said Mark, "quit stealing cookies. Mum blamed us."

"You steal them too," I said.

"Not yesterday," said Matthew. "Why should we get in trouble when we didn't even get to eat them?"

"All right, I'll tell her it was me. Big deal."

"Just—stop stealing them!" said Mark.

"Since when did you guys get so goody-goody? You can't tell me what to do."

"Okay, okay," said Matthew, shifting his weight on my legs. "Tell her about the other thing, Mark."

I tried to get up again, but Mark held my arms down and I didn't get anywhere.

"Second of all," said Mark, "we saw you with that Ghost Girl last night and we told her to leave you alone."

"What? It's none of your business who my friends are!"

"She's dangerous, Polly," said Matthew. A little frown creased his forehead. "She's going to hurt you."

This was too much. The twins were never this serious. They were always teasing and making fun of me. This had to be another trick. With an enormous heave I knocked them off and managed to sit up.

"Why can't you just leave me alone?" I asked furiously. "I don't want to play your stupid game!"

They looked at each other. "We're just trying to help, Pol," mumbled Mark. He looked upset.

"You don't realize," began Matthew, "you don't realize what she is. She can really, really hurt you. She wants to steal your soul. We don't want that."

"Yes," added Mark, "and we're not playing a trick, honest. That Ghost Girl is going to wreck everything."

I pushed off the covers and jumped out of bed. I must have startled Susie because she jerked and I think she bit her thumb.

She let out a wail, and the boys exchanged a look of alarm and then scurried out of the room.

I bent over the railing of the crib and patted her little back. She was wearing pink flannel snap-up PJs with the feet in them. She was warm and soft. I picked her up and gave her a hug. She put her arms around my neck. She smelled good.

"Olly," she gurgled.

I looked down at her in surprise. "Susie! You said my name! I didn't know you could talk."

She smiled at me and said it again. "Olly."

I hugged her again. Suddenly I felt a surge of something in my chest—not sure what—but it kind of hurt and made my eyes tingle.

"Susie," I whispered, putting her back in her crib. "You're a good baby, aren't you, Suze? No more crying?"

She shook her little head and put her thumb back in her mouth. She understood me! Weird! I know babies grow fast and learn things and change and all, but this was a first for Suze. Maybe she'd actually be a fun little sister one day. She seemed to like me, which was more than I could say for Lu, Moo or Goo.

I half expected my mother to appear after Susie's outburst, but the house remained still. The clock beside my bed said 5:30. I had time to go up to the attic before breakfast.

Rose

I woke up early. Something had been troubling me all night as I slept, and finally I swam to the surface to find out what it was.

I turned on the lamp. The room had an unreal, sort of blank look. The books and wallpaper and curtains I'd been waking up to every day were suddenly unfamiliar.

I sat up and tried to focus on what was it that had kept me tossing all night. Something that had happened last night, something different. The twins? Why were they so scared of me? But that wasn't it. The old lady? I'd seen her before.

But I'd never touched her. Last night was the first time I had ever touched a ghost. She didn't feel dead. She felt as real as Polly, or Kendrick, or the Horrors. What was happening to me? First the Door Jumper/Winnifred, who had to be the scariest ghost I'd ever encountered. And the first one to actually do some harm, apart from frightening me.

I'd met up with scary ghosts before. Like the skeletal old lady whose fingers kept falling off. I'd seen her last spring in a department store with my mother. We had gone shopping for an Easter dress, and every time I found a dress I liked the ghost would howl like a banshee and stretch out a finger to touch it—and then one of her fingers would fall off. This went on through about six dresses and six fingers, and then I couldn't bear it anymore and made my mother take me home.

And there were others, more terrifying. But although they frightened the wits out of me, they had never hurt me. The Door Jumper had done something to Polly, something serious.

I wondered if a ghost could actually kill a living person. In all the stories I'd read, if anyone died, it was from fear. Was that what the Door Jumper was trying to do? Scare Polly to death?

And then there was the old lady, so kind and so real. Who was she? How could I have actually touched her? Unless . . . unless Polly was right and I was a ghost myself.

No. I wasn't going to think about that. I threw back the covers and hunted up my slippers from under the bed. I needed to find out more about Winnifred. There were still unopened boxes in my grandmother's room.

SECRETS IN THE ATTIC

Polly

If anything, the attic was colder than usual. I was glad that I'd stopped to put on my woolly housecoat and warm slippers. I huddled under the blanket and put my head up against the wall, listening.

"Rose?" I called out. "Rose, are you there?"

It was all quiet next door. No creaking floorboards, no singing, no whirling Door Jumper. No earthquakes. My dream came back to me then, as clearly as when I was having it. I saw Rose with that awful look on her face, climbing out of the crack. I shuddered.

I wondered if the twins were right, that Rose was somehow dangerous and I wasn't seeing her properly.

I remembered how she'd hugged me last night on the doorstep and the worried look on her face as she'd told me go to bed early. She was the first real friend I'd made in ages. I didn't care if she was a girl or a ghost. Nobody was going to take her away from me. Not the twins, not the Door Jumper, not anybody.

Thinking about the Door Jumper—Winnifred—made me sit up. I flicked the flashlight around the corners. At least she wasn't in my attic. I wondered why she didn't just jump through the wall to get me. Maybe there was some kind of ghost rule where she couldn't leave the actual house she was haunting. Or maybe my house had something that kept her out.

I sank down again among the cushions and the blankets. I'd have to go down in a minute and start getting ready for school. I felt a curious heaviness, like I could stay there all day and snooze. The thought of getting to my feet and climbing down into my closet seemed like a tremendous effort . . . my eyes closed. It was very quiet.

The humming started very softly. I didn't pay much attention until the words started to form.

> *She's like the swallow that flies so high*
> *She's like the river that never runs dry*
> *She's like the sunshine on the lee shore*
> *She's lost her love and she'll love no more.*

I sat up, sleep dropping off me with the blanket.

"Rose?" I called out.

The singing stopped.

"Polly?" came her voice from behind the wall. "What are you doing up so early?"

"Uh . . . I had a bad dream . . ." I replied. I didn't want to tell her what the twins had said about her.

"About Winnifred?" asked Rose.

I didn't want to tell her about the dream, either.

"No, yes . . . oh, I don't know. It was scary anyway, and I woke up. Why are you up in the attic?"

"Oh . . . I just wanted to sit and think for a while."

"There's no sign of the Door Jump—I mean, Winnifred?" I asked.

"No. All clear."

We fell into silence.

"Polly?" said Rose finally.

"Yes?"

"Polly, I don't think it's a good idea for you to come back here. I think it's dangerous for you."

Dangerous. That's what the twins had said.

"Yeah. I guess you're right. But where can we meet? I can't sneak you into my house. There are always people around. Always."

Silence.

"Rose? Are you still there?"

"Yes."

"Look, Rose, I gotta go get ready for school. What about the library?"

"The library? What library?"

"The one on Parliament Street. We could meet there. After school."

"Oh. All right."

"At four o'clock?"

She took a while to answer. And when she did, it was as if she was speaking from a long, long way off.

"Oh . . . that's fine. Four. See you then."

She fell into silence again. I climbed down out of the attic back into my everyday life and left all the ghosts behind.

Rose

What Polly couldn't see through the wall that divided us was the wooden box that sat on the floor in front of me. I didn't want to tell her what I'd found because I knew she would want to come charging over, and I was determined to keep her out of harm's way.

I'd come across the box in one of the unopened cartons from my grandmother's closet. They were filled with old clothes, scarves and a collection of purses. In the last one, under a big red angora shawl, I found the box.

Locked. It was about the size of two shoe boxes laid side by side, made of wood that had a slightly red tinge to it. It had a band of darker wood near the top, covered with decorative carving.

There was a little keyhole but no key. One corner of the box had been dented, and in places the wood was scratched or discolored.

I knew it was important. I could feel it.

I had hauled the box up to the attic where I wouldn't be interrupted. And I'd been sitting looking at it, trying to figure out how to open it with no key, when Polly heard me singing. I hadn't even realized I was singing until she spoke, as if she was breaking a spell.

I had found it hard to focus on what Polly was saying. All I could think of was the box and the strange feelings I had when I looked at it. As if I'd seen it before. As if it held something precious that would somehow explain everything. It was almost as if the box was hypnotizing me—making me feel dreamy and sleepy. I wanted to get into it so badly, I could almost see breaking it open—if only it hadn't been so beautiful.

I could hear movement downstairs—Mother in the bathroom, probably. High time I was getting dressed. Reluctantly, I tucked the box out of sight under the chair. Then I climbed down the ladder to begin my day.

THE LIBRARY

Polly

Of course the Parliament Street Library is just about my favorite place in the whole world. A building full of books! What's not to love? There's a big old counter at the front where you check your books out, and then it opens up into this huge room, with windows all along one side looking out over Gerrard Street. In front of the windows are four long wooden tables with benches along each side. The tabletops are about a foot thick and so are the legs. I wouldn't want to have to move one of them. That's where you sit to read your books and fill out your cards for the ones you're taking home.

On the other side are floor-to-ceiling shelves full of books, and in between are rows of bookshelves. In the farthest corner from the door there is a fireplace, AND armchairs. I've never actually seen a fire there, but it doesn't take much to imagine one.

I went right to the fireplace and plonked myself down in a chair. This corner was hidden from the librarian at the front desk by the bookshelves, and it was quiet now. Strictly speaking, this was the adults' section of the library, but Mrs. Gardner, the librarian, didn't mind, and she let me take out grown-up books whenever I wanted. She liked me because I was there at least twice a week, and I took out lots of books and always brought them back on time. I liked to talk to her about them sometimes. She knew so much about books. I think I might want to be a librarian when I grow up, so I can spend all my time with books.

The children's section was way over on the other side of the library, through a door beside the counter. It was cozy too, with low tables and small chairs and lots of great books, but it was always full of noisy little kids.

Today Mrs. Gardner didn't even look up when I came in. She was busy checking out books for a mother with three little kids in tow.

Rose was late. She got off school way before me so I thought she'd beat me there. After a while I started to get bored, so I headed over to the children's section to see if there were any Philomena Faraday books I hadn't read yet.

The door to the children's room had a big window in it. I was just about to push the door open when I saw something inside that made me freeze. Mark and Matthew, heads bent over a book at the table in the center of the room. I backed up slowly and then scuttled back to the fireplace. Whew. Close call. The last thing I needed was them bugging me some more about Rose.

I must have just missed her as I walked across the library, because there she was, perched on the edge of one of the arm-chairs, in her dark cloak with the hood thrown back over her shoulders and her hair wild and everywhere. She looked like someone from another time, as if she had just stepped off a windy moor.

"Hey, Rose!" I said, bouncing up to her and grinning. She looked up. Her eyes were so dark. Dark and troubled. If anything, the shadows underneath them were even darker today.

"Hey, Polly," she replied with a wan little smile. "Sorry I'm late! I was . . . um . . . looking for something at home."

"No problem, but I think I should warn you, the Horrors are here."

She stood up and peered behind me.

"Where?"

"In the children's section. Don't worry, they probably won't come out here. Mrs. Gardner's been keeping a close eye on them ever since they built book towers and then knocked them over . . ."

"Oh. Okay. If you think it's safe."

She sat down in the chair but kept glancing over her shoulder, as if she thought they would jump out of the bookshelves at any moment.

"Why are you so worried about them, anyway?" I asked curiously.

"They make me nervous," she replied, examining her nails suddenly. "They call me Ghost Girl. I don't like that."

Hmmm. Something there. She wasn't going tell me, and I certainly wasn't going to tell her what they'd said to me that morning. I thought it better just to leave it for the moment.

"So, what's new?" I said, settling into a chair and putting my feet up on the low table. Mrs. Gardner wouldn't like that, but then Mrs. Gardner couldn't see me from the front desk. "What were you looking for that made you late?"

Rose smiled.

"You're going to love this, Polly," she said. "A key. A key to a secret box I found in my grandmother's room this morning."

Rose

I hadn't spent a lot of time at this library. My mother had brought me one Saturday after we moved in last summer and introduced me to the librarian so I could get access to the adult books. I'd been back a few times. I did like the quiet, secluded little corner by the fireplace. There were ghosts in the library, of course, but they were strangely contented, for ghosts, and I didn't mind them. Sometimes I wondered if they oozed out of the books. Today there was a little boy in dark wool knicker-bockers and a big cap who looked kind of hungry and shy. Something familiar about him. A character from Dickens? Or maybe a Parliament Street urchin from a hundred years ago? A young woman in an old-fashioned, long red dress stood gazing out the window, and a man in a black coat sat at a table, his work-worn hands turning the pages of a book with pictures.

They didn't bother me. What was bugging me was the thought of the twins just thirty yards away. If they saw me with Polly they might come after me again. I didn't want her to hear them accusing me of hurting her and putting her in danger. I felt bad enough about that already.

"Tell me about the box," said Polly breathlessly, pulling her feet off the table and sitting up straight. "What do you think is in it? Where do you think the key is? Did it belong to Winnifred? Do you think it has a secret compartment?"

"The whole box is a secret compartment until I figure out how to get it open," I replied. "I looked through my grandmother's dresser drawers, in her jewelry box, in my parents' bedroom, all through the drawers in the kitchen. I couldn't find a key that fit."

"It's got to be somewhere," said Polly. "Maybe she kept it in a hidden drawer in her dresser, or under a loose floorboard in her room, or inside a false book—"

"I could try the study . . ." I said doubtfully.

Polly jumped to her feet. "Come on, let's go look right now!" she said, shrugging on her coat and then pulling me along by the arm.

I grinned, in spite of myself. Ever-enthusiastic Polly, always ready to leap into the next adventure.

"Now wait a minute," I said. "I don't want you—"

"Not so fast," said a squeaky voice behind her.

"You're not going anywhere!" said another.

Polly whirled and there were the Horrors, blocking our way and looking as fierce as two grubby eight-year-old boys can when they're dressed in snowsuits and flap-eared caps. One of them was clutching a book and the other was pointing his finger at me.

THE DRUNKEN GHOSTS

Polly

Before I could open my mouth to tell them to get lost, a tall figure swept out from among the bookshelves and came to rest between me and the Horrors. It was Mrs. Gardner. She stood with her back to me and her hands on her hips.

"WHAT did I tell you about ever setting foot in the grown-ups' library again?" she demanded in a surprisingly loud voice.

The twins cowered. It brought joy to my heart to see them like that.

"We were just—" spluttered Matthew.

"We were only—" gasped Mark.

"OUT!" thundered Mrs. Gardner, advancing on them. "You've checked out your book so now you have no more business in this library. I'm going to phone your mother. You made a promise never to come into this section and . . ."

While she continued to lecture them fiercely, her back still to me, I beckoned to Rose and mouthed at her, COME ON, ROSE, LET'S GO!

She grabbed her coat and we slipped away. Soon we were heading up Parliament Street, past the scuzzy storefronts,

Woolworth's, Woman's Bakery . . . I looked longingly at the heaps of fresh buns, cookies and tarts in the window of the bakery, but Rose dragged me past it.

"The key, remember?" she said.

We turned down Winchester, crossing the street so we wouldn't have to walk past the Winchester Hotel. Rose moved quickly, casting nervous glances over her shoulder.

"Ghosts?" I inquired.

"Mmm," she replied. "You don't want to know what just came out of the hotel behind that guy with the filthy coat . . ."

Eeek.

Rose

What I saw coming out of the Winchester Hotel behind the tottering, boozy man in the long dirty coat was actually just another staggering drunk in a filthy coat, but both he and his coat hailed from a time when Victoria was Queen of England. Drunken ghosts didn't bother me much, but Winchester Street, lined with ancient, ramshackle rooming houses, had the distinct aura of a place where any number of questionable ghosts could appear at any moment.

Our way home led past the cemetery, but I knew a way to avoid it. I ducked down a side street and led Polly through a couple of back alleys that brought us to the corner of Sumach and Amelia. Our street was quiet. No ghosts. We stopped in front of Polly's house.

"You're not coming in with me," I said. "It's too dangerous. I can't predict what the Door Jumper will do."

"But—" Polly began.

"NO!" I said. "I told you this morning. We're not risking it."

"But I want to be there if you find the key. I want to see what's in the box," she pleaded. "Come on, Rose!"

"Polly—"

She clutched my arm. "Promise you won't open it without me, Rose. Promise!"

I tried to shake her off but she held firm.

"Oh, all right," I said finally. "Let's meet up in the attic after supper and I'll let you know if I've found the key. Then we can figure out where and when we can open it."

"Okay, but no peeking!" She flashed me a huge grin and ran into her house.

THE HIDDEN DOOR

Polly

After supper I slipped quietly up to my room. It was the twins' turn to help with the dishes, so all they could do was give me dirty looks as they cleared the table. I shut my bedroom door carefully, climbed up the ladder to the luggage loft and hoisted myself through the trapdoor into the attic.

I called out for Rose but there was no answer, so I curled up under the blanket and waited. You'd think if she'd found the blasted key she'd have come up right away so we could open the box. But maybe one of her parents had come home, or she had to practice the piano or something.

It was pretty boring sitting there. I flicked the flashlight around but the beam was so weak that I couldn't see much. Then I got up and started tapping the wall between the two attics. Don't know why. Except people always tapped walls in books and that's how they found secret passages.

I didn't discover anything except that a few spiders had lived there in years gone by. Sticky bits of spiderweb clung to my hand. I took a step back, turning the light up to the very top of the wall near the roof.

That's when I fell. I think I tripped on something, maybe *The Ghastly Ghost at My Gate*, which I'd forgotten about ever since that first time I heard Rose. I went sprawling and the light swung wildly across the room. I hit the floor with a thump, then I kind of bounced a couple of times. I hurt my head. And my back. And my leg, which twisted underneath me.

The cone of light from the flashlight came to rest, casting a sickly yellow glow into the far corner of the attic. I sat up with a groan, and as I bent to pick up the flashlight, I glanced along the path of light to the corner. The wall was different there. Strips of crisscrossed wood formed an X, framed by a square.

I took the light over to examine it more closely. I ran my fingers over the wood, then pulled.

The square of wall swung towards me. Beyond was darkness.

Rose

Kendrick stood just inside the front hall, glaring at me.

"You're late, and your supper is ready," she said with a disapproving sniff, then turned on her heel and disappeared into the kitchen.

My supper was laid out in the dining room, as usual. I picked at the chicken, had a few bites of mashed potatoes and left the peas. I tried a spoonful of chocolate pudding. It was surprisingly good, so I had another spoonful. And another. I was nearly at the bottom of the bowl when I realized what was happening—I was enjoying it! Was Polly's love affair with food rubbing off on me? I'd never finished a dessert before.

I headed into Father's study, thinking about the key. The room had a faint odor of damp wool, leather and books that reminded me of him. I sat down on his desk chair and spun slowly around. The books, the dark paintings, the old armchair by the fire all rotated past me. I spun a little faster, making them blur.

Winnifred had been in this very room, with her father. Perhaps she had spun in this chair. Perhaps she had breathed in that very booky smell and missed him too when he was away. I stopped myself by grabbing the desk and the room spun on for a moment or two and then straightened. I pulled opened the desk drawer.

Pens, erasers, pencils, a stack of creamy letter paper with crinkly edges, matching envelopes, a bottle of ink, some elastic bands, paper clips . . . all very tidy. Probably Grandfather's. I'd never seen my father use a fountain pen. But there were no stray keys.

I made a quick search of the other drawers in the desk but found nothing but files and papers. Then I got up and began examining the bookshelves. They looked normal, with an occasional framed photograph or small decorated box breaking up the long straight lines of books. None of the boxes held a key, and none of the photographs had a key taped to the back.

So where would someone hide a key in a room like this? Polly had said something about a false book, which seemed unlikely. Even if it was possible, how was I to know which book was false?

I went back to the desk and got down on the floor under the desk to see if I could find a secret compartment behind the drawer, but there was nothing, just the frame of the desk. I tucked up my legs and sat there for a while. I used to sit under my father's desk like that at the old house.

My tummy was very full of supper and I was feeling a bit sleepy. I closed my eyes.

I didn't fall asleep. I know I didn't. I just closed my eyes. But the room felt suddenly darker and I heard a rushing sound, like a train going by, and a long, agonized scream tore out of someone, and I was falling again, falling, and then it was me inside the scream, and I was calling for my father but he was too far away to ever hear me.

I jerked as I opened my eyes with a start and banged my head against the top of the desk. I crawled out and got to my feet, wondering if I had screamed out loud and if Kendrick would burst in, and I was turning towards the door when I stopped dead in my tracks.

Someone was sitting in the armchair by the fire.

THE SECRET PASSAGE

Polly

A door. A small door, to be sure, but nevertheless, a door.

I felt a bit like Alice in Wonderland bending down and peering in the door she was too big to get through. This door was about a foot and a half square. I flashed the light in, but all it revealed was the sloping roof meeting the floor.

I sat back on my heels and used the flashlight to examine this wall again. The roof angled down from the peak to about two feet above the floor, where it cut away and went straight down to meet the floor. I poked my head carefully inside the door and looked around the corner. There was a small passageway leading away into darkness. The builders must have wanted to close the attic off from the eaves.

But how far did it go? Could I possibly get into Rose's attic this way? Could I even fit?

I went back to the adjoining wall.

"Rose!" I called out. "Rose!"

No answer.

I went back to the door. If only there'd been a little bottle labeled "Drink Me," I could have shrunk myself down and made the whole thing a lot easier.

I took off my bulky sweater, gripped the flashlight firmly in my hand and crawled in.

It smelled different from the attic: a moldy, animal smell. I wondered if there were mice in there . . . or maybe something bigger, like a squirrel or a raccoon. I banged the flashlight against the wall a couple of times.

"Get lost, mice!" I called out. "Big scary person coming!"

I found I couldn't actually crawl on my hands and knees. I had to lie on my stomach and wriggle. I wished I hadn't had that second helping of mashed potatoes and gravy at supper. It was a tight fit.

It's hard to tell distance in the dark, especially when you're lying down and can't exactly measure by footsteps. But I got to about where I thought my house should end, and the passage kept on going. My flashlight sent out a dim yellow beam, and I could see only about three feet ahead. I carefully hauled myself along a little farther and then stopped and listened.

If I was in Rose's house now, I had no way of telling. All was silent, except for that distant hum of the city I could hear in my own attic. I lay still for a moment.

A strange feeling of peace descended on me. I was neither here nor there, and the world was going on without me. No one, absolutely no one, knew where I was. I felt tired and oddly warm there, squeezed under the roof. I could almost have drifted off to sleep, wrapped in the house, letting everything melt away into the dark.

I opened my eyes with a jerk. It was dark. Very dark. My flashlight had gone out.

Rose

It was my grandfather. He had died before I was born, but I knew him at once. There was a picture of him in a silver frame on the mantelpiece in the living room. He wore the same three-piece suit, with a gold watch chain linked across his vest and a stiff white shirt and dark tie. He had the same head of slightly wild gray hair. And the same stern, unsmiling expression on his face. But there were tears rolling down his cheeks.

I'd seen so many ghosts—some scary, some harmless, some funny—but all of them sad. Yet somehow, this one was the saddest. The feeling of grief weighed down the room, and I felt I could barely lift my foot to take a step towards him.

But I did. I had turned my back on ghost after despairing ghost. Ghost toddlers with pleading eyes, weeping women, frightened children, heartbroken old men—I had resisted them all. This one was different. My father's eyes stared at me from beneath my grandfather's bushy eyebrows, and his nose and mouth were strangely familiar. I realized with a shock it was because he looked like me.

"Grandfather?" I said, taking another step. "Grandfather? Don't cry."

Adults aren't supposed to cry. At least, not around children. I found I was completely unable to bear the tears of this stern, forbidding old ghost. Even though I had never met him alive, he was part of me. I bent down and took his hand. It felt bony and cool.

"Don't cry," I said again, peering into his face.

He looked at me then, but his eyes didn't focus.

"Winnie," he whispered, his voice cracking. "Winnie, I'm sorry. Forgive me."

"NEVER!"

The scream seemed to echo off the walls and around the house, as if a tornado swept into the room and then tore off over the cemetery. I didn't see Winnie but I knew it was her.

THE WHITE HAND

Polly

Backwards or forwards? I could wriggle backwards into my own attic and find some new batteries, maybe, and come back.

But I was so close. Maybe there was a door in Rose's attic like mine. She had said she'd come up after supper, so she'd be there soon. Maybe she had found the key and we could open the box together.

I crawled on. The floor was rough and scratchy beneath me. I was probably collecting a few slivers through my shirt. But I had to be nearly at the end by now.

Finally, my groping hand hit something ahead. The end of the house. I turned on my side and ran my fingers over the wall, looking for the door, pushing.

Nothing gave. I backed up a bit and pushed some more. The wall was solid.

Maybe there wasn't a door. For some reason this thought made me panic, and for the first time I felt the space closing in on me, and I had trouble catching my breath. I pushed blindly at the wall.

"Rose!" I called out. "Rose!"

Something moved under my fists, very slightly, and I threw all my weight at it.

"Rose!" I shouted, and the wall moved. Only a couple of inches, but I wedged my feet against the eaves and pushed with all my might and it edged open. I was just beginning to squeeze myself through the opening when I was suddenly struck with a splash of icy coldness that took my breath away, the way you feel when you jump into a freezing cold northern lake. As I gasped for air, I heard a rushing in my ears and a kind of hissing whisper.

"You are dead!" said a voice full of hatred.

Fingers of ice closed around my throat and the darkness grew even blacker. I tried to call out "Rose!" again, but my words were choked off and I winked into nothing.

Rose

My grandfather looked me right in the eyes.

"You've got to help her," he said and disappeared.

Just then I thought I heard Polly calling me. The room was silent and empty. Her voice seemed to be inside my head.

"Rose!" she called desperately.

I felt, rather than saw, Polly struggling for her life, choking, drowning, going down.

She was in the attic. I don't know how I knew, but I did. I ran up the stairs two at a time, burst through my grandmother's closed bedroom door and hurled myself into the closet and up the ladder.

I grabbed for the lamp and turned it on. There was no one there—the cardboard boxes were in a heap by the wall, my little nest of cushions on the stuffed chair looked undisturbed.

"Rose!" I heard Polly calling again in my head, from a long, long way away. Where could she be? I waded into the boxes and started pushing them aside. I stepped on something squishy and, to my horror, I realized it was a small, white hand. I pushed away the last boxes.

Polly was lying half in and half out of the wall, from which a square had somehow fallen open. Her face was white as clay.

"She's dead," came a voice behind me, and I whirled to see the girl in the long buttoned black dress. She was standing by the lamp, her hair lit up from behind. Her eyes were shadowed, but I had the strangest impression that I was looking at myself.

"No she isn't!" I yelled and fell to my knees. Polly felt cold to my touch.

I had learned mouth-to-mouth resuscitation at summer camp. I tipped Polly's head back, checked her mouth for obstructions and then breathed into her, turning my head between breaths to see if her chest was rising. Counting each breath, in and out.

It was textbook. I was good at it. I had won a badge.

Behind me I could feel the ghost watching.

"She's dead," she said again, a note of triumph in her voice. "You're wasting your time, you fool."

I took no notice and continued to breathe into Polly. I had never had a friend before. I wasn't going to lose her.

PART THREE

THE CURSE

Out flew the web and floated wide;
The mirror cracked from side to side;
"The curse is come upon me," cried
The Lady of Shalott.

ALFRED, LORD TENNYSON, "THE LADY OF SHALOTT"

BREATH

Polly

Everything was blank. Empty. I was very, very cold. But I couldn't see anything. I tried to lift my hand up in front of my face, but for some reason I couldn't move. I felt frozen. I tried to call out, but no words formed. Why couldn't I see? Was this a dream? Was I sick? I remembered a headache, a cool hand on my forehead.

I wanted my mother. A wave of longing for her swept over me. Why didn't she come?

Far away, someone was calling my name. I felt a whisper of something warm tickling inside my chest. Then pain shot through me as I took a breath.

Rose

I felt her start to breathe again. A tiny shudder. Then she was coughing and spluttering and trying to sit up. She looked scared.

I sat back on my heels.

"You're okay, Polly," I said. But she was looking at something over my shoulder.

I whirled around.

"I tell you," said the furious ghost in the black buttoned dress. "She is dead."

"No, she isn't," I spat at her. "You are! You get out of here and never come back. You're not wanted, you never were. Nobody loves you and nobody ever will. Don't you ever attack my friend again. If you do, I swear I'll—"

"What?" sneered the ghost. "Kill me?"

"YES!" I screamed and rushed towards her. She vanished.

MIRROR IMAGE

Polly

It was so weird. I woke up in the attic, coughing, and there was Rose with a white face leaning over me, and behind her I could see another girl who looked just like her, all dressed in black, and then Rose leaped to her feet and the two of them were arguing back and forth. It was like watching someone fighting with their image in a mirror. Then Rose screamed and the other girl disappeared.

I tried to get up but I was all wobbly. Rose came over and knelt down beside me.

"Are you okay, Polly?" she whispered.

"Yes, but—"

"She tried to kill you," Rose went on. "How did you get up here? I told you it was dangerous. Did you sneak in the front door?"

I tried to tell her about the passage, but I had another fit of coughing and so I just waved at the wall. The little door hung open, revealing a small black square.

Rose crawled over and peered into the darkness, then turned to me with shining eyes.

"You know what this means, Polly? Now I can get into your house too!"

Rose

The attic felt quite empty. Winnie had gone. For good, I hoped, but I doubted it. I went downstairs and got Polly a glass of water from the bathroom. It was funny that Kendrick hadn't appeared to investigate the screaming or running up the stairs. She must have heard the commotion, but I suppose she was doing her best to stick to her "Ignore Rose" policy.

Polly looked better after she drank some water. I held the glass for her because her hands were shaking.

"I saw her, Rose," she whispered. "This time I saw her."

"Your first ghost," I said, and my voice trembled. "What do you think of them now?"

"I see what you mean," said Polly, smiling a crooked little smile. "She wasn't much fun."

I smiled back, and a sudden sweet feeling of relief flooded through me. Polly was okay.

"Did you find the key to the box?" she asked, taking the glass in both hands and having another drink.

I shook my head. "No. I don't know where else to look." I didn't mention what had happened with my grandfather's ghost in the study. I would tell her, but not now. She still looked pale, and her hands shook when she held the water glass.

"Polly, why did you come? I told you to wait in your attic. I would have come soon."

She looked sheepish. "I know, Rose. I guess I just forgot everything else when I saw the secret passage. I couldn't resist! Could you, if you had found it?"

"Maybe not. But you can't come back here again."

She grinned weakly at me. "I won't argue with you."

"You'd better go home now. We can meet tomorrow and figure out what to do next, but I think we've had enough for today."

"Okay."

She turned to crawl into the passageway, then hesitated and looked back at me.

"Rose?" she said. "Would you mind coming along behind me? It's so dark."

"No, of course not. Just wait a minute while I get a flashlight."

I went silently down the stairs and into the kitchen. Kendrick's television was still droning from the basement. The flashlight was kept in the bottom drawer beside the sink. I slipped it out, tested it and went back upstairs.

Polly was sitting against the wall looking very tired. I waved the flashlight at her.

"Got it!" I said. "Let's go."

I followed her into the passageway. It was cramped but not too bad. Harder for Polly because she was bigger than me.

She stopped once, about halfway through.

"Polly?" I asked. "You okay?"

She was still for a minute.

"Polly!" I said more sharply, giving her ankle a shake. She roused herself then, apologized and continued to wiggle along.

I squeezed through the little door into her attic and looked around curiously. Just like mine, only empty and backwards. The trapdoor was at the opposite side.

Polly returned the flashlight to me and lowered herself through the door into a loft full of suitcases. I would have loved to go down and see her room, and maybe the baby, but not this time. Polly needed to rest. She looked up at me to say good-bye, her face pale and serious.

"Thank you, Rose," she said quietly. "For saving me. For a while I thought no one would ever come."

POOR GHOST

Polly

For a moment in the passageway I blanked out again. I felt heavy and sleepy and everything started to fade until I felt Rose behind me, shaking my foot. I took a deep breath and then I was okay.

After I said good-bye to Rose I got into my pajamas and fell into bed. I was so very tired. No wonder. That awful Ghost Girl had tried to choke me to death. I even wondered if I had been dead for a while, when everything was so white and I couldn't move. But Rose brought me back.

Rose. Her face swam into my mind, the way dream images do when you're just falling asleep. Her shadowed eyes, her crazy hair. She looked so much like that Ghost Girl. They could have been twins. But they felt like opposites.

Why did Winnifred hate me so much? The only reason I could think of was that she was jealous. I had Rose, but Winnifred had no one. I could understand that. I knew all about jealous.

It ate you up. It poisoned everything. It made me hate Susie, with her baby smell and her pink PJs, who never hurt anyone. It made me hate my brothers, because my parents paid more attention to them than to me. It made me hate Lu, because she was so much smarter and prettier than I'd ever be, and it made me hate Moo and Goo, because they took my father away from me. And finally, it made me hate myself for being so unpleasant and petty.

Yes, I knew all about jealous. Poor ghost.

Rose

After I shut the trapdoor on Polly I hesitated a minute or two. I knew I should get back home, but I wanted to have a look around her attic.

I walked over to a heap of blankets and pillows by the wall. That must have been where she was sitting the day she heard me singing.

I laughed. She must have been terrified. I'm not surprised she thought I was a ghost. This attic was spooky—way more spooky than mine. Because it was empty, I guess. My foot nudged something half-hidden in the blankets and I bent to pick it up.

It was a book: *The Ghastly Ghost at My Gate*. I sat down among the blankets and turned the flashlight on it. It had a creepy picture on the front of a house outlined against a moon-lit sky, with a tall iron gate in the foreground and a beautiful girl in a long cloak with a misty phantom swirling around her. I opened it up to a bookmarked page. I'd read a few books by Philomena Faraday and they were all similar. Her ghosts were usually the predictable Hollywood version who go about moaning and trying to kill the clueless heroine. Not at all like the ghosts I had met, although . . .

I sat up and skimmed the pages. This Gate Ghost did bear an uncanny resemblance to the Door Jumper. On a page where Polly had turned down the corner to mark her place, there was a description of the ghost jumping out from behind the gate and trying to strangle Amanda in much the same way that the Door Jumper had attacked Polly. Similar methodology, as my science teacher would say. Maybe the author did know a thing or two about ghosts. I turned to the back flap to see if there was anything interesting written about Philomena Faraday. Nothing much, just a few lines telling me she lived in New Hampshire with seven cats.

I noticed the little cardboard pocket glued inside the back cover, where libraries stick their cards. I glanced at the due date stamped there: April 10, 1963. Evidently Polly had squirreled this one away and never returned it. Polly must have had special privileges at that library.

I put the book down. Time to get home. I didn't like Polly's attic half so much as mine. It had an abandoned feeling. Sad. Almost as if there was a ghost here. I flicked the light around the four corners of the room, just to make sure, but there was nothing. I crawled into the wall and wiggled my way back to my own attic. As I straightened up and looked around at my cozy chair, books and the stacked cardboard cartons, I experienced a very unusual feeling: I felt like I was coming home.

SHORTBREAD

Polly

The next day after school Rose and I met in my attic. She brought an extra flashlight, a tin of Scottish shortbread and the box.

We turned both our lights on the box. It was certainly mysterious. The wood was smooth and worn. It must have been very old. It had a familiar smell. I bent down and breathed it in.

"Rose, it smells like roses. Don't you think that means something?"

"Nothing spooky about that," said Rose firmly. "It was in a box with my grandmother's shawl. All of her stuff smells like roses. It was her favorite perfume."

That was Rose's story. She had an answer for everything, but I wasn't convinced.

I munched on a shortbread (they were delicious!) while she told me about seeing her grandfather's ghost the day before. I nearly choked when she said, "And then I turned around and SOMEONE was sitting in the armchair." When Rose described how he had called out to his daughter, calling her Winnie and asking her to forgive him, I felt so bad for the poor old guy.

"We've got to help him," I said. "We've got to help him, and Winnie too."

Rose stared at me, and her mouth twisted a little in disapproval.

"She tried to kill you, Polly," she said. "Why do you want to help her?"

I shrugged. "She's not going anywhere. She'll be back, haunting you and trying to keep me out of your house. If we can figure out what happened to her, maybe we can help her stop being so mad."

Rose was silent, watching me. She looked like a ghost again, her face half lit by the glow from the flashlights, her hair fluffing out around her head.

"Don't you want to help her?" I asked finally.

Rose shook her head. "She wants me to. They all want me to help. All the ghosts. They never leave me alone, Polly."

"But your grandfather," I said softly. "You want to help him, don't you?"

"I suppose so."

Another long silence. Despite the brighter light, the shadows of the attic seemed to close around us. I imagined the darkness full of Rose's ghosts, clamoring for help, plucking at her hair. Plucking at my hair. I gave a little jump and then shook myself briefly, like a dog shaking off a drift of snowflakes.

"It must be awful," I said. "All those ghosts. All wanting something. Have you never helped any of them?"

Rose leaned towards me and spoke in a quick, fierce voice that I'd never heard before.

"What am I supposed to do?" she hissed at me. "I can't bring them back to life! I can't make anything right for them! I can't DO anything! But they still ask me. I just wish they'd all go away forever. I just wish I was normal, like you. With a normal family, like you. And no Door Jumpers and dead grandfathers and ghostly perfumes sighing in haunted rooms!"

Her face was twisted with fury, and she looked more like Winnifred than ever. I felt a cold shiver crawling up my spine. But I reached out and covered one of her shaking hands with mine.

"I'll help you, Rose. It'll be easier with two of us. We'll find the key and get Winnifred sorted out somehow, and then maybe we can find a way to get the ghosts to leave you alone."

She looked at me and started to laugh.

Rose

Polly looked so sweet as she reached out to me, blindly swearing to do the impossible. Even now, after being attacked by the Door Jumper and nearly dying, she still didn't have a clue. You can't just "fix" things. You can't just change the way the world is because you want to. She was such a child compared to me.

But that's why I liked her. She didn't know what might be lurking in the dark but she jumped in anyway, and she actually believed she could make a difference. So I laughed.

"All right," she said, dropping my hand and looking relieved that I wasn't raving anymore. "So, how are we going to find this key? Is there anywhere you haven't looked?"

"All kinds of places," I responded. "My parents' bedroom, the books in the living room, the dining room cupboards. The kitchen. Kendrick's flat. But it would take me hours to search the whole house."

"We have to use logic," said Polly with a little frown. "It's just a matter of elimination and logic. That's how the detectives figure things out in murder mysteries."

I rolled my eyes. Polly saw but chose to ignore it. She picked up the box and slowly turned it, examining each side.

"Okay," she said, peering at the strip of carved wood. "Okay. So if it was your box, what would you do with the key?"

"Put it in a drawer, a jewelry box, an envelope . . ."

"Right. And you've looked in your grandmother's dresser and her jewelry boxes?" asked Polly, shining her flashlight at the keyhole.

"Yes," I said impatiently. "Yes, I looked everywhere in her room."

"It must be a very small key," said Polly slowly. "Do you think maybe it was put on a chain?"

"There were no keys on chains in her jewelry box," I said impatiently. "I would have noticed."

"I wonder . . ." said Polly. "Would you have noticed if it was on a bracelet? A charm bracelet? My mum has one, and it has a little golden key on it. A bit too small for this box, but—"

I stopped frowning. "She did have a charm bracelet! She used to take it off and let me play with it when I was little. There was a silver book, and a musical note, and a little man . . . I don't remember a key."

Polly met my eyes. "Was it in the jewelry box?"

"I . . . I don't remember. There was a pile of chains and stuff, but no keys, so I didn't go through them all."

"Go!" said Polly.

THE CHRISTMAS PICTURE

Polly

There was no question of me going with Rose to look for the key. I didn't want to risk another encounter with Winnie. I listened as Rose bumped along the passage. Then there was silence. I tried to picture her scooting down the ladder into her grandmother's room, over to the dresser, opening the jewelry box. Either it was there or it wasn't. She'd be back soon.

It was funny how you really couldn't hear anything in the attic. Just that faraway hum, of traffic, maybe, or the city. It was soothing to lie back in the quiet and let my mind drift away.

"Got it!" said Rose, bursting through the little door. I must have fallen asleep for a minute because I hadn't heard her coming.

She held out a clinky silver charm bracelet to me. Sure enough, there was a little silver key. Trembling, she fitted it into the box. With a couple of twists, the box was open.

Rose

It was weird, the way Polly figured out where the key would be. Sometimes I wondered if she was psychic, after all. Even if she didn't see ghosts the way I did. Or maybe she was right and it is possible to live life as if it were all a game, or a story in a book. Whatever the reason, she knew exactly where to find that key.

As I lifted the lid of the box, a breath of my grandmother's rose perfume wafted out, and then it was gone. Polly and I leaned over the box, shining our flashlights on the contents.

The first thing we saw was a picture of me.

I picked it up. It was taken last Christmas, I thought. I was wearing a black velvet dress with buttons down the front and I was staring at the camera, unsmiling, my hair a dark cloud around my face. I was standing in front of my grandmother's sitting-room mantel, which was decorated with pine boughs and candles. The date printed on the bottom of the photograph read "December 1962."

The next thing in the box was a picture of Winnifred. It, too, was taken at Christmas, and she was wearing a black velvet dress much like mine, standing in front of the same decorated mantel. This photograph was undated, but she looked about my age.

"Wow," said Polly. "You two look like twins!"

She was right. I stared at the picture. I knew it wasn't me, because the dress was more old-fashioned and the photograph was yellow and faded with age, but otherwise we looked exactly the same. Our faces were the same shape and our noses, mouths and eyes were identical. Even our hair looked the same: wild and curly. But Winnie had a strange, haunted expression in her eyes.

"Polly, do my eyes look like that?" I whispered.

"Uh . . . sometimes," she said.

"Can you tell us apart?" I asked.

"Hmmm," she said, looking at the photographs again. "Not really. Except she looks kind of angry."

There were more pictures of Winnie and me at different ages, all taken at Christmas in front of that mantelpiece that never seemed to change.

"These are so weird," said Polly. "Do you remember your grandmother taking them?"

The Christmas photograph. Grandmother always made a big deal about it, after we opened our presents. I had to put on the new Christmas dress she gave me every year and stand in front of the fireplace. She tottered a bit the last few years, when it was hard for her to stand without support, but she still took the picture.

Afterwards she would smile gently at me and say, "Thank you, Rose. You look just lovely."

They were all here, matched up with identical photographs of Winnifred. I felt sick.

LOCK HER UP

Polly

"Why do you think she took them?" I asked Rose.

Rose sat very still, staring at the photographs.

"I don't know," she said finally. "Maybe to show how much we were alike? But she never said anything, not a word. I didn't even know I had an aunt."

"Do you think maybe she thought you WERE Winnifred, that you were reincarnated?"

Rose slapped the photos down on the floor and turned back to the box.

"Don't start that weird stuff again, Polly. I'm not Winnifred, all right? I'm me." She fished some papers out of the box and started going through them.

"Winnifred's birth certificate, birth notice in the paper . . ." she said.

"But what if your grandmother thought you were?" I insisted. "Winnifred, I mean. Since you looked so much alike?"

"My grandmother was a Presbyterian," Rose retorted. "They don't believe in reincarnation. Hey, look at this."

She handed me a scrap of paper that had been cut out of a newspaper. It was a death notice. We read it together.

DIED, Winnifred Rose McPherson, aged 13 years. Suddenly in Toronto, January 8, 1923. She is survived by her loving brother William, and parents Dr. and Mrs. Alastair McPherson. Funeral arrangements have not yet been made.

"That doesn't say much," I began, but Rose had turned back to the box and pulled out a letter typed on paper that was so thin you could almost see through it. We bent over it together.

Whitman Private Nursing Home
750 Lampert Street
Montreal, Quebec

December 20, 1922

Dear Dr. McPherson,

This letter is to acknowledge receipt of your cheque for $500.00. We will expect the arrival of your daughter, Winnifred Rose McPherson, on January 9. As agreed, she will remain here indefinitely, and we will invoice you each month for the cost of her care.

As you know, we specialize in patients with mental disturbances, and we are well equipped to make her comfortable. Please be assured we will exercise total discretion in the treatment of your daughter. Your privacy is our chief concern, and all our records will be kept confidential.

> *Yours sincerely,*
> *Dr. George Ferry*

"They were sending her away," I breathed. "To a mental hospital in Montreal."

Beside me Rose was very, very still.

I fumbled for the death certificate.

"She died on January 8, the day before she was supposed to go. Rose, what do you think happened? Why did she die?"

Rose

So that was it then. They thought Winnie was crazy. She saw ghosts, just like me. And they found out. And they were going to lock her up. But she died first.

"Something awful," I whispered. "Something terrible must have happened. That's why nobody talks about her. It's too horrible to even say."

"What could be too horrible to even say?" asked Polly.

"I don't know. I—I don't want to know." I started stuffing everything back in the box and closed it.

"I've got to go, Polly, I've got to get out of here. I can't breathe, it's too dark, it's—"

Polly grabbed my arm.

"Rose, it's okay, we can figure it out. Rose, don't go. Please. Calm down."

"Calm down?" I shouted. "I can't calm down, Polly. Don't you see? It's all happening again. Kendrick said she was just the same as me. My grandmother saw it. Winnie and me, we're the same. It's like we're the same person. We're both cursed. They tried to erase her, they tried to pretend she never existed, and then I was born and I'm just as crazy as she was and they leave me alone and no one ever pays attention to me and eventually, when they find out about the ghosts I see, they'll lock me up, but maybe something terrible will happen to me first and I'll die and then—"

I threw myself into the passageway, leaving Polly bleating behind me.

"Rose! Rose! Come back!"

THE BRIDGE

Polly

I could see why she was so upset. Winifred wasn't someone you wanted to take after. Yikes. And it was all so spooky, the way she looked just like Winnie, and saw ghosts just like Winnie, and how maybe her grandmother thought she was Winnie . . . and how did Winnie die, anyway?

Rose had dropped the papers she had been looking at on the floor. I tidied them back into the box and settled against the wall with the box on my lap. Maybe I'd find a clue.

The first thing I pulled out was a child's drawing of a bird with a forked tail. It was flying, and there were trees and houses far below. It was signed "WINNIE," in shaky block capitals. What's with the swallow? I wondered, and reached for the next paper. This was a typed letter, on letterhead from a school. St. Ursula's Academy. Rose's school. It was dated Tuesday, May 10, 1921.

Dear Dr. McPherson,

It is with great regret that I write to inform you of the recent decision taken by the Board of Governors.

*Unfortunately, we must deny your request that your
daughter Winnifred be reinstated as a day pupil at
the school.*

*We refer you to our letter of March 1, in which
we asked that you withdraw her from the school.
Her behavior since coming to St. Ursula's in January
has been disruptive and alarming to the other students.
She is either uncommunicative in the extreme or she
talks wildly to herself. Our school is not equipped to
handle this type of pupil. Her refusal to do her work
and her many absences make it impossible for her to
make any progress.*

*I understand your concerns about her education, but
I can only suggest you make private arrangements, since
she is so unsuited to spending time with other children.*

*Yours sincerely,
Doris Frost,
Headmistress*

Winnifred had gone to the same school as Rose. Mind
you, it didn't look like she went there very long. Kicked
out. For being weird. 1921—she must have been about eleven.
I wondered if she went to another school after that. I flipped
through the papers.

There were letters from five other schools, dated from
1917 to 1920. The first was the local public school, where I

went—Winchester School. The other four were private schools around the city. They all said they couldn't keep Winnifred because she was too quiet, too noisy, too disruptive, didn't do her work, didn't respect authority, was absent too often. The last letter was the one from St. Ursula's. A year and a half before she died.

And now Rose was a student at the same school. And she said everyone ignored her. All the time. As if she weren't there.

Rose

I felt as if I couldn't breathe. The walls were closing in on me. A pressure was building inside my chest that felt like it was going to burst. I scrambled through the passage as fast as I could, hurled myself down the ladder, through my grandmother's room, down the stairs and out the door, stopping only to grab my cloak. I wanted to get far, far away from that house.

I ran all the way up the street and around the corner. I didn't know where I was going, but the cold air filling my lungs eased the pressure inside, and I wasn't going to stop till I had to. I passed a few people muffled against the cold, hurrying home, but I paid them no attention.

Finally, about five blocks farther, I stopped. I leaned over, panting, trying to catch my breath. When I raised my head I took in where I was. A deserted stretch of Parliament Street, beside St. James's Cemetery. This was an even bigger cemetery than the one behind my house. A tall iron fence was all that separated me from the tombstones looming in the darkness.

A feeling of dread gripped me. I took off running again, even though my lungs were burning and my legs felt like jelly. A dark figure flitted along the sidewalk, far ahead of me, but I couldn't make out if it was alive or dead. I had a tingly feeling on the back of my neck. I looked over my shoulder. Another dark figure was moving quickly along behind me. Following me.

I kept running. Round the corner, across the Rosedale Valley Bridge, the shadowy figures keeping pace with me. Then I stumbled.

I caught myself before I fell and stood with my chest heaving, taking deep, ragged breaths. I looked back along the bridge. The following shadow was still there, standing about two hundred feet away, not moving. I looked forward. The dark figure ahead was also motionless.

I began to walk. Both shadows also started to move at the same slow pace. I tried running again. Both figures sped up. Then I walked. They slowed down. This was just weird. If they were ghosts, what were they playing at?

By this time we were moving along the Bloor Viaduct, the big bridge that spanned the valley. I started to feel oddly light-headed and suddenly much colder. It began to snow. It's too early for snow, I thought, looking up at the fat white flakes drifting down from the dark sky. There wasn't much traffic on the bridge, but a few cars swished past me, their lights blurring. My dizziness increased, and I blinked. Maybe there was some kind of motor show going on, I thought, because the cars all looked like the old-fashioned kind, with square bodies and huge fenders.

The lampposts spread little circles of light for a few feet around them, with patches of darkness in between. Before me, the dark figure moved steadily along, moving in and out of the light. Behind me, the shadow kept pace. The snow was thicker now, obscuring my vision.

Suddenly the dark figure ahead disappeared. One minute it was there—the next it was gone. I whirled around to see if the shadow was still there.

The sidewalk behind me was empty. I was alone on that vast bridge that stretched on before and behind me into darkness.

THE SWALLOW

Polly

I rooted around in the box. There were lots more drawings of swallows. They were all signed by Winnie, and judging by how her signature changed, they were done over a number of years. The earlier drawings were simple, a child's drawings, but gradually they got a lot better. She was really quite good, I thought, looking at one of a swallow perched on the side of a nest. The nest was built under the eaves of a house, and I could see the heads of two little baby birds peeking over the top.

There must have been thirty drawings of swallows in that box. Pencil, crayon, watercolors. There were more of the nest and many of the swallow flying. In the colored ones, the swallow's feathers were carefully painted cool blue, its throat orange and its breast white. As Winnie grew older, the pictures became more and more detailed, down to the last feather on the swallow's forked tail. One of the pictures of the nest showed the cemetery wall and the tops of gravestones, making it clear that Winnie was sitting at her window, drawing the swallow that returned to its nest year after year.

I noticed that in every picture where the swallow was flying, it was passing over a different landscape. The earlier drawings showed trees made of bubbles and sticks, rolling hills and square houses with triangle roofs. But as the form of the swallow improved, the countryside became more intricate. And it changed. A thick pine forest, a mountain range, a desert island, a tropical jungle, icebergs, ocean—Winnie's swallow was traveling the world.

Rose

I felt suspended in time and space on that high bridge, far from the dim city lights. I moved as if I were in a dream, one foot after another. The blowing snow felt cold on my face. A few more of the old-fashioned cars trundled by, their engines loud. A stone alcove opened up at my right, jutting out into space. I turned in and leaned against the cold stone parapet. Darkness opened up around me—the big sky, the long drop to the valley below.

Cursed. My family was cursed. First Winnie, now me. It had killed her. Was it going to kill me too? Or—was I already dead, as Polly kept saying? Was there a chance that I really was Winnie? That all my life, everything I could remember, was just some pale dream I was having in the shadowy world of the dead? Was the reason why I could see ghosts the simple fact that I was a ghost myself?

I drew a deep breath of cold air into my lungs. How could that be? How could I be dead and still see these cloudy puffs of warm breath come out of me? How could I be dead and feel the tingling cold in my fingers and the bitter wind on my cheeks, the snow softly falling on my eyelashes?

"Easy," whispered a voice in my ear. "You could be dead and imagining it all."

I whirled around but there was no one there. I heard someone laughing, and then a loud thump, as if a car had hit something, and then suddenly I was caught in a dizzy, whirling black cloud, with that sensation I'd had in the graveyard of falling, lights tumbling around me, the scream—and then it stopped.

I was crouched on the cold concrete sidewalk beside the balustrade. Someone was standing in front of me. In the light from passing cars I could see black oxfords, dark stockings, a long black dress.

I raised my head.

Winnie stood there, staring down at me. Looking like my twin.

THE BOY

Polly

The first time I'd met Rose she was singing a song about a swallow. Her dead aunt drew swallows over and over again.

Rose went to St. Ursula's. Her dead aunt got kicked out of St. Ursula's.

Rose saw ghosts everywhere. So did Winnie.

They thought Winnie was crazy. Rose was terrified of going crazy.

They looked EXACTLY ALIKE.

It couldn't all be coincidence.

I wondered where Rose had got to. I hoped she was okay. I didn't know how to help her, except to keep investigating.

I had no idea of the time. I was probably late for dinner. I stuffed the drawings back in the box and left it in the attic. If Rose came back, she would find it.

Rose

The passing cars and the noises of the city faded away and there was only Winnie and me, face-to-face on the bridge. It was like looking into a mirror. My mouth, my eyes, my hair. A wild look in her eyes.

I opened my mouth to speak but no words came out. I swallowed and tried again.

"Why have you brought me here? What's going on?"

She took a step towards me. I took a step back.

"You need to know," she hissed at me. "You need to understand."

"Why is it snowing in October?" I demanded. "Why are the cars and the streetlights all old-fashioned? What have you done to me?"

"I haven't done anything," she said. "You are following in my footsteps. You have always been following in my footsteps, and now it's time for you to understand why."

"I'm not!" I protested. "I'm not following in anyone's footsteps. I won't! I'm going home." I whirled around and started to run.

I only made it out of the alcove, back to the sidewalk, and then I stopped. The shadowy figure that had pursued me all along Parliament Street and across the bridge stood a few feet away, staring through me at Winnie.

It was a little boy dressed in a long wool coat, with a cap pulled low on his forehead and a scarf wound tight around his neck. But I would have recognized those eyes anywhere—whether they were looking out at me from a photograph from forty years ago, or twinkling at me as he said good night on those rare occasions when he was home at bedtime. My father.

THE ACCIDENT

Polly

Nobody seemed to notice that I was late for supper. There was some big discussion going on about the twins and the library. Apparently Mrs. Gardner had called Mum to complain about them being in the adults' section yesterday. I grinned at them as Dad was reaming them out, and they both scowled back at me. I scarfed down my dinner, for once happy not to be noticed.

After dinner I thought maybe I'd go to the attic and see if Rose was around. But just as I had one foot on the bottom rung of the ladder to the luggage loft, I heard the twins at my door.

"Polly?" called Mark. "We want to talk to you!"

There was no use going up. They'd just come after me. I poked my head out of the closet.

"What?"

They were crowded together in the doorway, shuffling their feet and looking worried. What was with those two? Matthew clutched a picture book.

"Can we come in?" said Mark.

"What do you want?"

"Just let us come in for a minute to talk," said Matthew. "We want to show you something."

"Oh, all right," I said and flounced down on the bed. "What's bugging you guys? You're acting really weird, even for you."

They exchanged looks and then came and sat beside me. Matthew laid the book carefully on his knees.

"We want to show you this book, Pol," he said. "We got it from the library yesterday. We've had it out before. It's about ghosts."

"Oh?" I said, taking a look at it for the first time. It was called *The Ghost Girl and Other Tales from China*. It had a dark-red cover with a picture of a girl standing beside a Chinese pagoda. She had long black hair and a pale face. I took the book from Matthew and looked more closely at it. The twins watched me.

"She looks like Rose," I said. The girl's hair was straight, not curly, and she was Chinese, but there was something about the way she stood, the way her head was tilted, her sharp little chin that reminded me of Rose. The most striking thing was the girl's expression: her eyes, smudged with dark shadows, had that same haunted, desperately sad look I'd seen so many times.

"We thought so too," said Mark. "We think Rose is the Ghost Girl."

Rose

I turned back to Winnie, who was staring at the boy, her face twisted as if she were in terrible pain.

"I didn't want to hurt him," said Winnie in a broken voice. "I never wanted to hurt him. I didn't mean to, no matter what Father said." Tears rolled down her cheeks.

I looked over my shoulder. The boy was motionless, still staring at her, his face blank. A few cars whizzed by.

I turned back to Winnie. "What do you mean, 'hurt him'? What did your father say?"

"He said I was a danger to Willie. A danger to all of them. But it wasn't my fault!"

"Then whose fault was it?" I demanded.

She grabbed me by the arms and gave me a shake.

"It was the ghosts! You know! You've seen them!"

I tried to break loose, but her grip was strong. Strong and icy cold.

"You know what it's like! They never, ever left me alone. Day and night, everywhere I went. I didn't have a minute's peace. They taunted me. I screamed, I threw things at them. But nothing worked. It got worse and worse. I got so angry, everything went black. I hurt . . . people. Mother. Willie. Kendrick. When I threw things."

I finally shook her off and took a couple of steps away from her.

"So they knew?" I asked. "Your parents. They knew you saw ghosts?"

"No!" she yelled. "They didn't believe me! They thought it was all in my mind. Father was ashamed of me. He didn't want any of his doctor friends to know he had a child who saw things that weren't there. That's why he arranged to send me away. Forever."

"So what happened?" I asked. "That night? What happened to you and what happened to my father?" I glanced over at him.

The figure of the little boy still stood there motionless, as if frozen in time, staring at his sister.

She took a step towards me, her eyes gleaming in the light from the lamppost.

"It was an accident," she said. "It wasn't my fault. I didn't know he would follow me!"

"What happened?" I insisted.

Her eyes were fixed on mine, boring into me. "I had to get out of there. I was scared. I didn't want to be sent to Montreal. I couldn't breathe. I felt the walls closing in on me. I had to get out . . ."

Just the way I'd felt tonight.

"I ran. I didn't know where I was going, I just ran. It was cold. It started to snow."

Just like tonight.

"I got on the bridge here and I couldn't see anything. It was all white with snow. And there was a road barrier, for some construction work being done on the bridge, and I walked around it, and a car came sliding towards me and—" She stopped, staring at me, her dark eyes huge in her white face.

"It hit me," she whispered, "and knocked me through the barrier . . . and . . . and I fell."

The thump. The long free-fall through the air, tumbling over and over. The scream.

I could feel it. I could see it, just the same as if it were happening to me. The same way I felt it in the cemetery, and in my house, and here on the bridge a few moments ago. I gasped for breath and felt suddenly dizzy. I flung out my arm to steady myself against the parapet. The darkness beyond the bridge dropped away, into nothing.

I looked over at the boy. His face was a mask of horror. A scream formed on his lips but he made no sound. The snow kept falling, blanketing him in thick white flakes.

Winnie grabbed me again, her icy fingers digging deep into my arms.

"You've got to help me," she begged in a hoarse voice. "You've got to help Willie."

MAKE IT STOP

Polly

"Is that why you call her Ghost Girl?" I asked. "Because of this book?"

Matthew nodded. "She is the Ghost Girl, Polly. She looks just like her, and she floats around haunting people and—"

I opened the book. "What's the story about?"

"It's about this girl," said Mark. "She lives with her family, and everyone thinks she is alive but really she is dead. She lives like that for years and years and nobody ever figures out. But all the kids she makes friends with—they—they—"

"She steals their souls!" said Mark. "She feeds on their souls and makes them dead like her. Then those kids are ghost girls too, and ghost boys, walking around the world, and everyone thinks they're alive but really they're dead."

"It's horrible, Polly! We don't want that to happen to you. Don't talk to her!" said Matthew. "She's too dangerous."

I turned the pages and looked at the pictures. They showed the girl playing with one child after another in lonely spots. Then there were pictures of the children back with their families, eating dinner, being tucked into bed, going to school—but now they all had the same haunted, mournful eyes of the Ghost Girl. I shivered.

"It's just a story," I said. "It's not real. Rose is not a Ghost Girl."

Mark shook his head.

"That's what we thought at first, Polly, when we got this book out from the library a few weeks ago. We thought it was just a really cool fairy tale. But then when we noticed Rose one day, she has the same eyes, right? So we went back and got the book again and read it all over again. She's a Ghost Girl, Polly."

I started to laugh but it didn't come out right.

"Rose is nice, really she is. She just looks a little . . . strange. But she cares about me. She doesn't want to hurt me."

"That's how the Ghost Girl tricks you," said Matthew, pulling at my sleeve. "She makes you think you're her friend. Then she steals your soul. You gotta stay away from her, Polly!"

"I think this book is too scary for you," I said, standing up. "I'm going to tell Mum that you shouldn't be allowed to take it out of the library anymore."

"No! No!" they both said at once, reaching for the book and pulling it away from me.

"Don't tell Mum," said Matthew. "She'll ruin everything."

"Look, you guys are really scared," I said. "Mum should know."

They looked at each other and some kind of silent twin communication took place. Mark turned to me.

"If you tell Mum about the book," he said, "we'll tell her you've been in the attic."

Rose

"Let me go!" I yelled, and with an enormous effort I pulled myself away from Winnie's grasping hands. I took a couple of steps away from her, until my back was up against the stone cold wall. Willie stood to my left, still staring at his sister. His face was blank again.

I stood panting, watching her. She was looking at Willie as if her heart would break. For some reason I noticed that she had the same lock of hair falling loose in front of her face that I had, the one that refused to stay behind my ear.

She turned back to me. "Please," she said in a strangled voice, as if it caused her physical pain to say that word. "You're the only one who can help."

And there it was. Her eyes had that same beseeching, sorrow-drenched look I had seen on countless ghosts throughout the years.

"What can I do?" I cried. "Why do you even ask me? You know I can't help you. You're dead. There's nothing to be done."

"You can help," she replied. "You can make it stop."

"Make what stop?"

She took a step nearer, reaching out her arms in a gesture that took in the heavily falling snow, the sky, the bridge and Willie.

"This! Me! Everything! The ghosts. Me going on and on in that house, endlessly trapped in misery! I can't get out, Rose. I'm stuck there, in that place, in that time, in that night. It never ends for me, Rose."

She began to cry, great wracking sobs.

"I can't leave. Willie can't leave. My mother and father can't leave. We're all stuck in that awful night, that accident."

The image of my grandfather sitting in his study, tears rolling down his cheeks, came to me. And the sigh and the smell of roses in my grandmother's bedroom. And the pictures she took of me every Christmas, making me look like Winnie. I took a deep breath.

"My father can leave. He leaves all the time. He's never home."

"Look at him!" she said, pointing to her little brother, who stood frozen like a statue, only his eyes alive, staring at her. "Don't you see? It doesn't matter how far he goes, that night is always inside him. He's here on the bridge in that nightmare with me. Our whole family is locked in that night. It never got fixed. None of us can go until . . . until . . ." She stopped.

"Until what?"

"Until you go to Willie and tell him I'm sorry, that it wasn't his fault I fell, that he couldn't have saved me. Get him to let go of it and let go of me."

I stared at her.

"Go to my father? Tell him I saw his dead sister on a bridge and she wants me to tell him she's sorry? Are you crazy?"

"You have to tell him," she replied. "It's the only way to make it stop."

"Why do I have to tell him? What's it got to do with me?"

"You can see me. He can't."

She wanted the impossible.

"What do you think is going to happen once I tell him?"

"He'll forgive me. He'll let me go."

"NO!" I yelled. "He won't believe me. If I tell my father that his dead sister has a message for him, there's only one thing that's going to happen. Don't you see, Winnie? I'm just like you! As soon as they find out I see ghosts they'll lock me up!"

"Make it stop," she said. "Tell Willie. Then I can rest."

"You don't get it," I said fiercely. "I don't care about you. I don't care if you're trapped in that house. I don't feel sorry for you. When I look at you I see . . ."

What did I see? Myself. Everything I hated about myself. The hair, the pale face, the twisted features, the weirdness, the no-friends, the loneliness and the ghosts.

"Make it stop," she said again and blinked out. One second she and Willie were there and the next they were gone. I was staring into empty space.

FADING AWAY

Polly

It figured they knew about the attic. They were such sneaky, creepy, snooping little brats. If they told Mum, that would be it for me and Rose. At least, it would be the end of her being my secret friend. If our parents let us play together, we could still be friends. That is—I looked back at the Ghost Girl on the cover of the book—that is, if Rose was not a ghost. If she was—well, then how would I see her or talk to her if I couldn't get into the attic?

The Horrors were watching me as all this went through my mind. Matthew still had that anxious look but Mark was smirking. He knew he had me.

"All right, all right," I said. "But I'm keeping the book."

Mark started to object but Matthew pulled at his sleeve.

"Let her," he said. "She can read all about it, and then she'll know she has to keep away from the Ghost Girl."

I rolled my eyes. "Will you stop already?"

"She IS the Ghost Girl," said Matthew. "We see her all the time at the window next door, in the back bedroom, just staring out at the graveyard. She sits there for hours, Polly. She's a ghost, we know she is."

"And we've heard you talking to her in the attic," said Mark. "Lots of times. We've been in the loft, listening. That's how we know you go up into the attic."

"And we want to come up too," put in Matthew. "We want to see it."

This was quickly getting out of hand. My last refuge in the house, invaded by the Horrors.

"I'll tell you what," I said, standing up and shaking my fist at them. "You set one foot—one foot!—in that attic, or you breathe one word—one word!—of this to Mum, and I'll set the Ghost Girl on you! I'll help her get you and grab you and steal your miserable souls and then you'll be dead, DEAD, DEAD!!!"

They yelped and ran out of the room. Then they yelped again as I heard my mother accost them in the hall.

"Mark?" She sounded really mad. "Matthew? What have I told you about playing in Polly's room?"

"But Mum," started Mark, "she—"

"No excuses! You are not to go in there. Ever."

They grumbled and protested as she shepherded them downstairs. I grinned and flopped down on my bed. It was about time she came down on them for trespassing. I opened the *The Ghost Girl* and began to read.

Rose

For a moment I stood, frozen, staring blankly at the empty place where Winnie and my father had been a second before.

Then, as I turned to look over the balustrade, the world exploded in sound around me. All the noises that had been silenced when I was in that strange, muffled place with Winnie suddenly clattered into life. Cars thundered by, horns tooted, the wind sighed, and I thought I heard a scream dying away in the distance—but it might have been a car screeching its brakes or a far-off ambulance siren. The snow had stopped.

I couldn't see anything when I looked over the edge. It was deep black. The wind cut through my cloak. I was hungry and very, very tired. I turned away from the darkness beneath the bridge and headed home. As I walked slowly back along the bridge, I noted that the cars were normal 1960s cars, not the old-fashioned kind I'd seen in the snowstorm.

I did my best to push all thoughts of Winnie and my dad away. I told myself she was just another ghost wanting something from me that I couldn't give.

When I finally got home, Kendrick stood in the hall with her arms folded, as if she'd been waiting for me.

"You're late for dinner," she said. "You've kept me from my programs, worrying about you."

"Sorry," I mumbled, hanging up my cloak. I swayed with tiredness. Kendrick gave me a sharp look.

"Your mother called an hour ago. I couldn't find you so she gave me a message."

"What?" I said.

"She's staying at your gran's tonight. She's going over figures with your granddad, she said, for some early meeting at the factory tomorrow, so it's easier for her to stay there."

I felt the familiar letdown. I hated it when she didn't come home. It happened every couple of weeks. With Father still away, I'd be alone in the house, except for Kendrick snoring in the basement. Tonight of all nights.

I stumbled into the dining room and sat down at my place. Kendrick came in with a plate that had been in the oven. Pork chops and mashed potatoes, all kind of dried up at the edges. I pushed it aside and put my head down on my folded arms.

When was the last time my mother had hugged me? Or my father? When I was in the hospital in the summer? When I came home? I couldn't honestly remember. They were fading away from me.

LET THE DEAD STAY DEAD

Polly

The story about the Ghost Girl was much as the twins had described it. She looked like a live girl and no one knew she was really a ghost. She lured children away from their parents and stole their souls. They became like her, leading normal lives on the outside, but inside they were dead. They, too, had the power to steal the souls of other children, and so it went, the world filling up with hundreds of these horrible little zombie-vampires.

The pictures were really creepy, and the more I looked at her, the more the Ghost Girl looked like Rose. It was strange that with all the ghost books I'd read I'd never seen this one.

I closed the book. Rose's face stared up at me from the cover.

Rose

I heard someone come into the room behind me and I sat up quickly, brushing away my tears. Kendrick moved over to the table and looked down at the untouched dinner.

"You need to eat something," she said gruffly, and she laid down a dish of custard and applesauce.

Usually Kendrick didn't bother with whether or not I ate my dinner, beyond a dirty look now and then when I left the food untouched.

I took a bite of the custard. It was really good: the custard creamy and the applesauce tart. She stood and watched me as I ate it, making me nervous. But I enjoyed it anyway and ran my finger around the bowl and licked it to get the last bits out. I knew that would annoy her. I looked up.

As expected, she was frowning.

"Where were you?" she asked.

"Just out," I replied. This was getting peculiar. She didn't usually ask me anything, but then, I'd never been out this late before.

"You shouldn't be out in the dark. Your mother wouldn't like it."

"My mother isn't here."

She picked up the plate of food and the empty bowl and started towards the kitchen.

"Kendrick?" I asked. She turned back to me.

"Were you here? The night Winnie died?"

The dishes clattered to the floor, the pork chops and mashed potatoes sliding off the plate with a splat. Kendrick ignored them and just stared at me.

"What happened?" I insisted. "Tell me."

She swayed and then reached for a chair and sat down heavily.

"You know?" she said.

"Yes. I know. Please tell me what happened."

Kendrick shook her head.

"It's not my place. Your father should tell you."

"My father isn't here. He's never here. I've got to know. Tell me!"

Kendrick took a long look at me, clenching and unclenching her fists in her lap.

"All right. But don't you ever tell your father it was me who told you."

"Why? Why is it such a secret?" I asked.

"Some things are better not talked about. They're too hard. Nobody in this house ever talked about what happened that night to—to—Winnie."

That was the first time she had spoken Winnie's name, and she spat it out at the end of the sentence, almost against her will.

"Everything that girl did brought trouble to this house. She was cursed from the first day she took breath."

"Cursed?" The custard was turning into a hard little brick in my stomach.

"Call it what you like. She was always uncanny. Caused her mother no end of grief, all her life. After she . . . died . . . I thought her mother would die from sorrow."

"What happened?"

Kendrick gave a long sigh, thinking back. "We didn't know they were gone. We thought they were both asleep in their beds. It was well after midnight when the police came to the door with Willie. I've never seen a child look like that, before or since—white as a ghost, trembling, icy cold—and all he kept saying over and over was, 'Winnie's gone, she's gone.'"

Her eyes had a far-off look, as if she'd traveled back in time to that dreadful night. She didn't look at me while she talked, and she kept wringing her apron in her hands, the words tumbling out as if she'd held them in for a long, long time and now could finally let them go.

"The police told us there'd been a car accident and Winnie had been knocked off the bridge, and the boy had seen it all. He was in some kind of shock. We packed him off to bed with hot water bottles, but he fell sick anyway and we nearly lost him too." She shook her head. "His mother was as white as he was, and for days she didn't speak, just sat there beside his bed, holding his hand. His father was not much better. This house was as silent as the grave. It was as if they were all ghosts. I kept cooking meals for people who wouldn't eat. That went on for months, even after Willie got better."

She seemed to come back into the present and fixed me with a baleful look. "It was all her fault! She brought a curse down on this house. One more day and she would have been gone off to hospital and we could have lived a normal life. But not that one. She had to go running off into the night and taking Willie with her and then getting herself killed and—" Kendrick stopped and took a deep breath.

"Your father was never the same after that. And your grandmother was never quite right either. Your grandfather—he never smiled again. It was bad before, with Winnie having fits and throwing things—"

Kendrick pushed her hair back from her forehead and leaned towards me. "See that?" she said, pointing to a thin scar along her hairline. "She did that. With a milk jug. She was wild. But it was worse, afterwards. Everyone was broken."

"My father? Was he broken too?"

Kendrick nodded. "He went quiet. Everything was quiet. For years."

She gave herself a shake and seemed to notice the broken plate and the food on the floor for the first time.

"And now you've come, stirring everything up again."

She stood up and eyed me with a return of her usual disapproval.

"Let the dead stay dead," she said. "Let them rest."

PART FOUR

THE SECRET

So runs my dream: but what am I?
An infant crying in the night;
An infant crying for the light;
And with no language but a cry.

ALFRED, LORD TENNYSON, "IN MEMORIAM"

DREAMING

Polly

That night, after I read the Ghost Girl book, I was lying in bed after lights-out. I could hear the soft rumble of Mum and Dad downstairs talking by the fire in the living room. The sound of their conversation went up and down, up and down. I dreamed I was floating on the ocean, and their voices became part of the rocking, gentle waves that rolled me along on an endless sea. I felt all my worries about Rose and the Ghost Girl and Winnie float away into the dark sea below me and the blue sky above.

Then a bigger wave rolled me down deeper and my parents' voices faded away. I thought I'd never reach the bottom of that wave, it was so very deep—and then somehow I must have, because I was moving upward again. This wave was so high I thought I would never reach the top—but suddenly I did, and for a moment I could see the ocean stretching on and on forever around me, and then I was heading down the other side of the steep, deep wave.

I wasn't scared. The ocean was rocking me, just like my mother, rocking me to sleep.

Rose

With everything that had happened, I thought I wouldn't be able to sleep, but I was so tired I went out like a light as soon as I crawled into bed. For a long time, I was just gone.

Then I had a dream. At least, I think it was a dream. I was alone in a place with no moon, no stars. It was cold. There was a wind blowing up from far away, a low rumble that grew louder and stronger until it was roaring around me, flattening my pajamas against my legs, whipping my hair around my face. I felt large things rushing by me in the dark. Cars, maybe? But they showed no lights.

"I'm lost," said a voice suddenly in my ear. A sad voice, a frightened voice, a familiar voice.

Immediately I was awake.

"Polly?" I whispered. I actually thought she was there in the room with me, her voice had been so clear. Except—was it Polly's voice? There was something strange about it. It could almost have been a little boy's voice. "Willie?"

There was no answer. It must have been very late. The house had that stillness that comes with the middle of the night. I lay there for a minute, catching my breath. My heart was pounding.

I was scared, but I didn't know why. I wrapped my arms around my shoulders and started rocking myself back and forth, the way I used to do when I was little and couldn't get to sleep.

"Mother," I said softly, wishing she were there.

THE HAUNTED SCHOOLYARD

Polly

The morning after my dream about the ocean, I couldn't concentrate at school. I kept thinking of Winnie's drawings of her swallow—flying over mountains, soaring over the sea, swooping up, spinning down—free. And yet, all the time when she was drawing those pictures, Winnie was cooped up in her house, year after year, unable to go to school, unable to make friends, just sitting at the window, drawing and watching for the real swallow to return to its nest every spring.

I straggled out behind the other kids at lunchtime, not looking forward to the long walk home through the gray streets in the cold wind. By the time I reached the gate, the schoolyard was empty.

"Hi, Polly," said a voice right behind me, making me jump.

I turned. Rose stood there, smiling. I don't know where she came from. I'd have sworn she wasn't there when I came through the gate. She was wearing that long dark cloak, and she looked like some fairy creature, with her dark, shadowed eyes and thin face.

"Did I scare you?" she said, laughing.

"Yes, you scared me!" I replied. "Where were you hiding?"

"I was standing right here, and you walked by me like you were a million miles away," said Rose. "What were you thinking about?"

"The swallow," I answered. "Winnie's swallow."

"What swallow?" asked Rose.

"Oh, right, you didn't see the drawings. You ran out so fast last night. What happened? Are you okay?" Then I stopped and stared at her. "But wait a minute, what are you doing here? Why aren't you at school? How did you get here? Why didn't I see you?"

I hated to bring it up again, but it was kind of spooky the way she wasn't there and then suddenly she was there. Just like a g-h-o-s-t.

"I don't have school today," she said, falling into step beside me as we went down the steps to the sidewalk and headed along Winchester Street. "There's a teachers' meeting or conference or something. And I was standing right here the whole time you were crossing the schoolyard. It's not my fault you're wandering around in a daze and didn't see me. It doesn't mean I'm a ghost."

"All right, all right," I said. "Sorry. I'm really glad to see you. I have a lot to tell you."

"So do I," she said. "Wait till you hear. I know how Winnie died. I know everything."

Rose

Polly looked so startled when I spoke to her at the schoolyard gate. It was really rather funny, the way she jumped and caught her breath. Exactly as if she'd seen a ghost. I'd been waiting at the gate forever while all these kids streamed by, ignoring me. For a while I thought maybe Polly wasn't at school that day, but then finally she appeared, huddled into her coat, walking slowly, her eyes dreamy.

We walked home together and I told her about Winnie and my father and the bridge. I was careful to lead Polly away from the cemetery and through my alley shortcuts. Polly's eyes were wide, and she kept jumping around whenever I got to the exciting parts and interrupting and grabbing my arm and saying, "Really?" all the time.

"You're going to help him, right?" said Polly when I'd finished. "You're going to help him and Winnie so she can fly away with her swallow and . . ."

Her voice died away as she saw the expression on my face.

"Rose?" she said uncertainly. "Rose?"

I shook my head. I couldn't speak. All I could see was that little boy, standing on the bridge with that lost, frozen expression on his face.

Polly reached out and gave my shoulder a little pat.

"Rose," she said again. "It will be okay. I know it."

"I want to help him, Polly, I want to help him more than anything in the world, but I'm scared to. If I tell my father I see ghosts he'll—he'll—Polly, he won't believe me. He'll think I'm just like Winnie."

"You don't know that, Rose. He might surprise you. Maybe all these years he's just been waiting for someone to help him and you're the only one who can."

"This could all be a trick!" I cried. "I don't trust Winnie. She tried to kill you, and now she's trying to get me locked up like she was going to be. She can't stand anyone being happy. She's bitter and twisted and—"

"Rose, you need to see the pictures she drew of the swallow. You'll understand her better. She must have been so lonely and unhappy, all those years in that house, with no friends, seeing ghosts all the time. It's no wonder she got so angry."

"What pictures? What's this swallow you keep talking about?" And then Polly told me.

By that time we had reached Polly's house and we stood shivering in the cold. I didn't want to leave her and go back into my lonely, empty house. Polly's eyes were bright with concern, and her cheeks were red from the cold. Wisps of hair were escaping from her hat and blowing around.

I shook my head. "I don't know. I don't see what difference a few drawings make. Winnie's still a crazy ghost."

She smiled at me.

"I'll bring you your grandmother's box after lunch," she said. "Then you can see for yourself."

MRS. LACEY

Polly

Rose was watching for me from her living room window after lunch. She waved at me to wait, and a minute later she was out on the street beside me, wrapped in her cloak.

"Here," I said, handing her one of my mother's striped cotton market bags with the wooden box tucked safely inside. "I gotta run, Rose, I'm late for school. No one was home so I had to make my own sandwich. I don't know where my mother is. But she did make a chocolate cake this morning," I added, grinning. "I put a big hunk of it in there for you too."

Rose smiled. "Yes, Polly, I can see you had some chocolate cake. It's all over your face."

"Ooops!" I wiped my mouth with the back of my sleeve. "Meet me after school in my attic?"

Rose's face fell. "I can't, Polly. I can't go in there again. Not after last night. Finding Winnie's death notice, and that letter from the hospital—it was horrible. I couldn't breathe—I couldn't—"

"No problem, Rose," I interrupted, hopping from one foot to the other in the cold. "We can meet at the library again. Bring the box. Gotta go!" and I ran down the street.

I dashed around the corner and then I had to slow to a walk. I was puffing like anything. Five minutes or ten minutes late, it didn't matter now. I'd get a note to take home to Mum either way.

As I hurried along the deserted streets I started thinking about Winnie. It made sense that she wanted Rose to help. In so many of the ghost stories I had read, ghosts would get stuck in something when they died—anger, sorrow, fear—and they were trapped there until they found the way out. They all wanted to move on to the next stage, whatever that was. Heaven, I guess.

I looked up as I crossed the road and that's when I saw them. My mother and Susie. They were on the opposite side. Mum was pushing Susie in the stroller. The basket underneath was stuffed with shopping bags.

I thought of nipping around the corner to hide. At least that would delay the lecture about being late for school.

It wasn't necessary. They didn't see me. Susie was babbling away and Mum was laughing and talking to her.

I stood on the corner and watched them pass down the street. Mum's voice gradually faded as they got farther and farther away.

I had never felt so lonely in all my life.

Rose

I watched Polly run down the street and disappear around the corner. Even though it was freezing, I didn't want to go back into the house. Kendrick kept watching me with her dark, suspicious eyes, as if I were going to turn into a witch and fly away on a broomstick.

I sat down on Polly's front steps and put the bag down beside me. I peeked inside and drew out something wrapped in wax paper—an enormous piece of gooey chocolate cake. Two layers, with lots of thick icing in between and on top. I took a bite. It was really good. Mrs. Lacey's chocolate cake was a lot better than Kendrick's. I took another bite.

Then I just sat there, huddled in my cloak, absently eating the cake while I thought about my dilemma. No matter what Polly said, I didn't see what difference it would make to look at a bunch of pictures of birds. I didn't trust Winnie for a minute. I pushed the image of the boy on the bridge away. Why should I have to fix everything? Didn't I have enough problems of my own, plagued by ghosts night and day? Although I hadn't seen any recently, except for Winnie. I looked around nervously.

It was okay. I was alone. Except for a woman coming down the street, pushing a stroller. I watched her idly. Didn't look like a ghost. She had a red coat on and glasses. She looked like—she looked an awful lot like Polly.

By the time I realized who she was and stood up to make my getaway, it was too late. She stopped the stroller in front of the house and looked up at me quizzically.

I tried to hide the bag under my cloak.

"Can I help you?" she said, approaching me. "Are you—?" She broke off, taking a closer look. "Oh," she said. "You must be the Ghost Girl. The one the twins talk about."

I didn't say anything. I just stood there, looking at her. It was very weird. She looked so much like Polly. She was chubby and had the same brown hair and a kind of bounce to her and—just like Polly—her words seemed to tumble out of her mouth without her stopping to think what effect they might have.

Mrs. Lacey laughed. Polly's laugh. "They shouldn't call you that—I'm sorry if they've been teasing you. They're awful boys, really. They'll be the death of me. What's your name?"

"Rose," I croaked. She glanced at the striped shopping bags in the basket under the stroller and then looked back at me, frowning.

"Rose, is that one of my bags you have under your cloak?"

Great. Slowly I took it out.

"I didn't steal it," I said stiffly.

She reached for the bag and looked inside.

"What's this?" she asked, pulling out the box.

I took it from her. "It's mine. You can keep the bag."

"Yes, I suppose I can. It's my bag. I made it myself. How did you get a hold of it? Is this something to do with the twins?"

I didn't want to get Polly in trouble.

"No. I . . . umm . . ."

The baby got tired of this and started yelling.

"Oh my goodness," said Mrs. Lacey, lifting her out of the stroller.

I took the opportunity to head back to my house.

"I'll be talking to your mother about this," called Mrs. Lacey as I ducked through my door.

THE DESERTED LIBRARY

Polly

The library was empty. I couldn't find Rose. She wasn't at the tables by the window, she wasn't in the comfy chairs by the fireplace, and she wasn't in the children's section. There was nobody there. Nobody at all.

It didn't feel right. I kept worrying about why Mrs. Gardner wasn't at the front desk. Someone could come in and steal a book.

I flopped down on my favorite chair by the fireplace and leaned my head back until I was looking straight up at the ceiling. That's when I realized the lights were off. What was going on? Some kind of a power blackout? Or maybe a fire alarm before I came?

I stood up quickly and was turning to head for the door when something caught my eye. A piece of paper with a drawing on it was lying on the floor, half under the opposite chair. A drawing that looked familiar.

I picked it up. It was one of Winnie's swallow pictures, with the swallow soaring through the air, its blue feathers spread wide.

So Rose had been here.

Rose

There was no sign of the librarian or Polly when I walked into the library. The place seemed strangely empty. I thought I heard a murmur of voices from the children's section, but I didn't investigate. I wanted to be alone.

I still hadn't looked in the box. After seeing Mrs. Lacey I'd gone up to my room and lain down on my bed and stared at the ceiling, worrying. There was going to be trouble about that bag. The grown-ups were going to find out about Polly and me being friends. If my mother said I couldn't see Polly, what would I do? My one friend. And if Winnie kept haunting me and trying to get me to talk to my father about ghosts—I closed my eyes. It was all too much.

I didn't think it was possible for a person to fall asleep in the middle of being worried to death, but I must have been tired, still, from all my adventures of the night before. The next thing I knew I was waking up and the light had changed and it was time to go to the library to meet Polly. I rushed out, afraid that I would be late, but when I got there Polly was nowhere to be found.

I headed towards the chairs by the fire and sat down, the box on my lap. I stared at it.

I didn't want to open it. I didn't want to see Winnie's drawings of the swallow. I didn't want anything to do with her.

I closed my eyes for a moment and saw her the way she had last appeared to me on the bridge. Her hair flying out around her face, her sad ghost eyes begging me to help her, her face so much like my own.

Everything inside me wanted to take that box and throw it under a streetcar. If I helped her, all the years I'd spent hiding would be over. My parents would know why I was so quiet, why I didn't sleep, why I had no appetite, and why I hated living beside a cemetery. They would know that I saw ghosts. I'd be packed off to the psychiatrists before I could blink, and they would lock me up, just like Winnie.

Or maybe . . . maybe Polly was right. Maybe there was a way through it. Maybe they wouldn't think I was crazy. Maybe they would help me get away from the ghosts. Maybe they would understand.

I opened my eyes and looked at the box again. In spite of myself, I opened it.

Inside were the drawings Polly had told me about. The one lying on top was of a beautiful blue swallow, soaring through the sky, its forked tail spread wide.

THE GHASTLY GHOST AT MY GATE

Polly

As I stood there, staring at the drawing, I thought I heard something. Voices, coming from far away, like a radio that's on a couple of floors below you. Maybe Mrs. Gardner was in the children's section with the door shut, doing a story hour. I stuffed the drawing into my book bag and crossed to the door that led into the other part of the library.

I couldn't see anyone in there. And the voices sounded farther away now, like they were coming from the basement. Did the library even have a basement?

I pushed open the door and went in. The tables were all smaller in here, closer to the floor, with kindergarten-sized chairs. Some picture books were spread open on them, as if someone had been looking at them but got up and left in a hurry. The lights were off in here too.

Weird. Very weird. I wandered past the displays and thought how small everything looked now compared to when I was little and had a hard time reaching the top shelf.

Now I could hear voices coming from the adults' section. Maybe Mrs. Gardner had come back.

I turned to head out and stopped short. The Horrors were standing in the doorway, staring at me.

Rose

The swallow was beautiful—its back a brilliant blue, its wings and tail feathers gray, a tiny band of yellow around its neck. It had been done in watercolors, with pale washes of different blues in the sky. There was no ground visible, just endless blue.

Polly was right. Winnie was really good at this. Each feather was detailed and perfect. The swallow looked as though it could go on flying forever.

I reached into the box and pulled out another drawing, this one in pencil, of baby swallows in the nest, all with their beaks open, hungry. The next drawing had the swallow flying high above an intricate country landscape—rolling hills, little houses, trees.

Sitting in the quiet library, I went through the pictures one by one. They showed me a part of Winnie I had never imagined. I dug in the bottom of the box to see if there were any more. The newspaper clippings and the letters were there, and something else, right at the bottom, something heavy. A book.

I pulled it out.

"Do you like ghost stories?" said a voice behind me. I jumped up and the book and the drawings and the clippings and the box all fell in a heap on the floor.

The librarian, Mrs. Gardner, was standing there. I don't know where she came from. I hadn't heard a thing.

"Oh, I'm sorry, I've startled you," she said. "Let me help."

We both got down on our knees and began picking up the mess.

"What beautiful drawings," she said, looking at the pictures. "Did you do these?"

"No, I can't draw at all. It was my—my aunt."

"Well, she's very talented. Do you like birds? I'm sure I could find you some really interesting bird books. That's a swallow, isn't it?"

"Yes." I scrambled to grab the clippings so she wouldn't be able to read them.

"Did you know swallows are a symbol of hope, all over the world?" she said, looking at another picture. "It's because they always come back, often to the same nest, year after year. They're a sign of spring."

"Mmmm," I said. Mrs. Gardner was very friendly but I wanted to get away from her. In a minute she was going to notice how weird I was, and that familiar look was going to cross her face, and she was going to start treating me funny.

"I . . . I should get going," I said.

"Don't forget your ghost book," said Mrs. Gardner with a smile, picking up the book I had pulled out of the box. It was Polly's book, *The Ghastly Ghost at My Gate*. Polly must have scooped it up in the attic and put it in the box by mistake.

"I guess you'll need to check it out," she said, flipping automatically to the back cover where the library pocket was.

"Oh, my," she said. "This is overdue."

She looked up at me suspiciously.

"April 10?" she said. "That's eight months overdue."

"Oh, uh, it's not mine," I said, knowing how lame that sounded. "It's—it's a friend's book."

Mrs. Gardner's friendliness was quickly turning to frost.

"Let's just check the records, shall we?" she said, her mouth set in a grim line.

I trailed behind her to the desk. Even her back looked cross. Librarians really hate it when your books are overdue. Polly was going to have to pay a big fine.

There was still no one around. I'd never seen the library so deserted.

Mrs. Gardner hauled out a drawer under the counter and started flipping through some cards that were arranged in rows.

"Faraday, Faraday," she murmured to herself. "Now why does that name ring a bell? Aha, here it is."

She held it up.

"Show me your library card, please," she said.

"I don't have it," I replied. "It's at home."

She gave me another stern look. "You came to the library without your card?"

Now she was really giving me the once-over, taking in my cloak and my wild hair.

"I didn't know I was coming here . . ." I faltered.

Her eyes narrowed.

"Shouldn't you be in school?"

"I . . . uh . . . I had the day off today."

She didn't look convinced. She peered at me.

"Wait a minute. I know you. Didn't I meet you last summer, with your mother, when you moved into the area?"

"Yes," I mumbled.

"And you've been in a few times since—"

"Yes," I mumbled again. I just wanted to get out of there.

"But if you moved here in the summer, why do you have a book that was due in April?"

"I told you. It's my friend's book. It got into my box by mistake."

"What's your friend's name?" asked Mrs. Gardner.

"I need to go," I said and scooted out the door.

"HUNT POLLY"

Polly

"Polly," said Mark. "You need to come home."

"No, I don't," I said. "I'm meeting Rose here.

Matthew shook his head.

"No, she's gone."

"Come with us, Polly," said Mark. "Mum wants you home."

Matthew shot a look at him. I knew that look.

"You just made that up, Mark," I said.

Mark turned on Matthew.

"What did you do that for, Matt? I nearly had her."

"Sorry," said Matt. "Didn't mean to."

"What do you mean, you 'nearly had' me? Why are you following me around? Are you playing some kind of 'Hunt Polly' game? Are you trying to capture me? You gotta be kidding, right?"

I walked towards them. They backed out the door.

"Just come," said Mark. "You don't need the Ghost Girl. You can play with us."

"You guys are just kids. I don't want to play with you. And anyway, Rose is not the Ghost Girl. She just looks a bit like her, that's all."

I followed them out into the adults' section. It was still deserted. But I could hear the distant voices, as if they were coming from behind closed doors somewhere.

"Do you guys know what's going on? Why the lights are out and there's nobody here?"

They exchanged one of those twin looks again.

"You can't see anyone?" said Matthew.

"There's no one to see. Why isn't Mrs. Gardner here?"

Mark's eyes swiveled over to the librarian's desk and then back to me. Matthew gave him a little dig in the ribs.

"Never mind her," said Mark. "Come on home, Polly. Ghost Girl isn't here."

"Oh, all right," I said and followed them out the door.

Rose

I ran till I was about a block away from the library and then slowed to a walk. I shouldn't have taken off like that. It wouldn't make any difference. Mrs. Gardner would find out it was Polly's book as soon as she matched up the numbers in her card catalog. Then she'd call Polly's mother, and probably my mother too, and we'd be in more trouble than ever.

I hurried along Parliament Street, clutching the box under my cloak. It was getting dark already. I couldn't think where Polly could be, unless she had to stay after school for some reason.

As I walked through the dim gray streets I thought about Winnie and her swallow, and the way she'd looked on the bridge the night before, and my grandfather's ghost, sitting in his study, begging me to help her. And my father, with that lost little boy inside of him, watching his sister fall off the bridge, over and over again.

Maybe . . . maybe I could give him Winnie's message. What if she was right, and I could put an end to all the ghosts in that house, and my father's misery? But would he believe me?

People brushed past me in the dusk. Everyone was in a hurry and no one paid any attention to me, as usual.

I was invisible.

FOOTSTEPS

Polly

I never walk with the twins. When we leave for school, they're either ahead of me or behind me. They ignore me and I ignore them. Unless they want to torment me about something.

But this time they stuck to me like glue, all the way home, one on each side of me. I guess it was part of this "Hunt Polly" game they were playing. When we got to the cemetery, I started to slow down, hoping to see some ghosts, but they each grabbed one of my arms and started to hurry me along the street, almost running.

"Stop it!" I said, trying to break free, but they wouldn't let go. They kept looking over their shoulders at the cemetery and acting kind of nervous.

"What is wrong with you guys?" I said, still trying to pull away. "What are you scared of? Ghosts?"

I was kidding, but they looked even more nervous, and Matthew said, "Yes," in a small voice.

Mark gave him a dirty look.

"Wait a minute, you guys can see ghosts?" I said, finally shaking my arms free.

"Yes," said Matthew. "That's how we can see the Ghost Girl. No one else can see her. Except you."

"Come on," said Mark, grabbing my arm again. "Let's get out of here. They're coming, Polly."

I stopped and peered through the iron railings. "I don't see anything."

"No, Polly!" said Mark. "They're dangerous. Please. Come on."

They both looked so scared that I stopped struggling and let them rush me along. We turned the corner to our street and slowed down.

"What do you mean, no one else sees Rose?" I asked.

They exchanged a twin look.

"Have you ever seen her talking to anyone else?" said Mark.

"Well . . . no . . . except Kendrick. I've heard her talking to Kendrick. Their housekeeper."

"What housekeeper?" said Matthew.

"You know, that old lady who's lived there forever," I said.

"She died," said Mark.

"Last spring," said Matthew.

Rose

As I turned down the last block to our street, I heard footsteps behind me.

I glanced over my shoulder. The light was so dim, I could

barely make out the tall, dark figure that was approaching, moving much faster than me and quickly catching up.

I stepped behind a tree and hid, holding my breath.

The figure stopped just before it reached my tree. It stood there for a moment. Then it spoke.

"Rosie," it said in a broken voice. My father's voice.

What was he doing here? I thought he was in Montreal.

I peeked out around the other side of the tree. His face was illuminated by a streetlight. He looked tired, and his shoulders were slumped, as if he were carrying a great weight.

"Winnie," he said and covered his face with his hands.

I moved carefully back into the shadows.

THE WITCH

Polly

"Wait a minute," I said. "Which old lady are you talking about? You must be thinking of Rose's grandmother. She died last spring. Kendrick is the housekeeper. She's always coming in and out carrying groceries."

Another twin look.

"Oh, that one," said Matthew. "She's scary. She comes out and yells at us if we even put one foot inside their backyard."

"Well," I said, "she may be scary, but she's not a ghost, and I've heard Rose talking to her, so that proves that—"

"That proves nothing, Polly," said Mark. "That old lady could be a witch, and witches can see ghosts!"

"She's a witch for sure," said Matthew. "Look at her eyes sometime. They're all small and beady, and I bet she puts spells on people who go in her backyard and—"

"Stop!" I cried. "Enough with the witches! Rose is my friend and she won't hurt me, ghost or no ghost."

"She is definitely a ghost," said Mark stubbornly. "We see her sitting at the back window for hours, just staring out. And no one ever sees her or speaks to her, except you and us. She's invisible."

"And if you see her talking to someone, it must be someone who can see ghosts," piped up Matthew.

"Like us," said Mark.

I stared at them. "How long have you two been able to see ghosts? How come you never told me?"

Another twin look.

"A while," said Matt. "Just a while. We don't like ghosts like you do. We don't wanna see them, do we, Mark?"

"No," said Mark carefully.

We'd reached our house.

"I think I'll just go call on Rose," I said. "Ghost Girl or not, she was supposed to meet me and I want to see if she's all right."

"NO!" said both of the boys. "You've got to stay away from her, Polly!"

Just then my mother stuck her head out the front door.

"There you are! Where have you two boys been? I told you to come straight home from school. You've got Cubs in fifteen minutes. We can just make it if we leave now."

"But, Mum—" whined Matt.

"We can't—" said Mark.

"In here, right now, no arguments," she said firmly. "And I'd like you to tell me what happened to the chocolate cake I left on the counter."

"Cake?" said Matthew, looking at his brother. "What cake?"

I laughed. Mark shot me a look as they headed up the stairs.

"Stay away from her, Polly," whispered Mark over his shoulder. "You don't understand."

Rose

I waited till I heard my father's footsteps fade away and then started slowly after him. My stomach felt funny. Why had he said "Rosie" like that, as if it hurt him to say my name? And then "Winnie," right after?

I could see the lights of cars crossing the Bloor Viaduct through the bare trees. I bent my head so I wouldn't have to look at them. The box seemed strangely warm and heavy in my arms.

Polly's house was dark. That was strange. It always seemed to be the center of various activities, day or night.

I walked up my front steps and opened the door. The house was very still. Quiet. As if no one was home. The light in the hallway was dim, and deep shadows filled the corners. My head felt light, the way it had on the bridge the night before. I seemed to be floating across the hall, making no sound. It was as if I had no control over my body but was just moving along a path that was laid out before me. I put the box down on the hall table as I passed and then stopped in the doorway to my father's study.

My father was sitting slumped at his desk, staring blindly into space. My breath caught in my throat at the sight of his face, which was etched with lines of care and distress I had never seen there before.

A movement behind him caught my eye. It was Winnie, stepping out of the shadows. She was wearing her long black dress with the white collar and staring at my father with that same hungry, longing look that I recognized from the eyes of every ghost I had ever seen. The look that always made me run.

EMPTY

Polly

I glanced at Rose's house. There was no sign of life. Where was she?

I decided on a bold move and walked up her steps to ring the doorbell. If Kendrick answered it, I could say I was taking orders for Girl Guide cookies. And I could study her very carefully and try to figure out whether or not she was a witch.

No one came. I knocked, hard.

Still no answer.

I tried the door. It was locked.

I wandered back to my house. Nobody was home. Mum must have taken the twins to Cubs, but I had no idea where everyone else was.

An empty house, twice in one day. Unbelievable! I sat myself down by the window in the sitting room where I could watch for Rose coming home. It was pretty dark out there, but a streetlight cast a small pool of light on the sidewalk.

It was nice to just sit there in the quiet house, with nobody bothering me. I didn't have to hide away to be alone. I had the whole house to be alone in.

Rose

Winnie raised her head and our eyes met.

It was just like on the bridge: I could have been looking into a mirror. Winnie reflected everything I was—lonely, weird, angry—but hungry more than anything else. A hungry ghost. Not hungry for food, like the Breakfast Ghost. Hungry for something else.

I no longer had a choice. I took a deep breath. "I'll do it," I said.

EGGS

Polly

My head hurt. It was like the ghost of a headache: a faint throbbing behind my eyes. It reminded me of something. I closed my eyes for a moment.

Eggs. It reminded me of eggs.

Rose

My father looked up at the sound of my voice.

"Rosie?" he said, frowning. "Is that you?" He peered at me.

The desk lamp made a little island of light around him, but the rest of the room was in shadows.

"Winnie?" he whispered. "Rose?" He passed his hand over his forehead. "For a moment I thought . . ."

Now even he couldn't tell the difference.

I stood in front of him, the box held tight to my chest. I felt like I did when I was little, before I learned how to talk. I opened my mouth but no sound came.

My father waited, looking at me.

I felt as if I was standing at the edge of a cliff and my father was far away, on the other side of the gulf. How was I going to get to him, except by jumping?

THE MESSAGE

Polly

That stupid fight with my father, about the eggs. Or the lack of eggs, to be precise. That was the day I had the headache, the day I met Rose. It seemed so long ago now.

I sighed. The circle of light on the sidewalk was empty. No Rose.

The ghost of the headache was getting stronger. And now my stomach felt sick. Another echo: the day I had that awful headache, my stomach was upset too.

There was something tickling at the back of my mind. Some memory to do with the headache and feeling sick. What happened that day? I tried to remember, but the headache was making my mind fuzzy.

I had gone up to the loft after Dad blew his top and ordered me to leave the breakfast table. I was hungry at first, because I hadn't eaten, but then I felt sick. I went to sleep in the loft and when I woke up, the twins were looking for me. And that's when I went up to the attic for the first time and heard Rose singing.

Rose

"It's about Winnie," I said. My voice was cracked and scratchy, as if I hadn't used it before.

"What did you say?" asked my father.

"Winnie," I said, louder this time. "I've got a message for you. From her."

There it was, right in front of me, all over his face, just as I'd expected. He thought I had lost it. His mouth fell open, his eyes popped and he looked wildly about the room, as if there was someone there who could help him understand. And all the time Winnie stood behind him, unseen and silent.

"I've seen her," I continued, a little more loudly still. "Your dead sister. I've seen her—her ghost."

He gaped at me.

"I see ghosts, Dad," I said, louder still. "I see them all the time. Just like Winnie did."

He started shaking his head back and forth.

"No," he whispered. "No!"

"Yes!" I was almost yelling now. I had to get it out. No matter what he did after, I had to get it out. "I see ghosts. And Winnie needs me to give you this message, because you can't see her, and I can."

He kept shaking his head.

"No—Rosie—don't—please." His words came out in little jerks.

"I have to. She can't rest. And you can't rest. And I can't rest. And nobody can rest in this house until you let her go.

She's sorry. She's sorry about everything. She's sorry about the accident, she's sorry she hurt you. But none of it was your fault and you have to let her go now."

My father just kept staring at me in horror, just as if—as if I were a ghost.

FORGOTTEN

Polly

No. That's not the way it happened. The twins weren't there when I woke up.

The white pool of light on the sidewalk seemed to be throbbing along with my headache. It grew bigger, then smaller. I closed my eyes.

Nobody was home that morning. The house was empty, the way it was now. They'd all gone away. Mum had taken the kids to the St. Lawrence Market, the way she did every Saturday, everyone trailing after her with homemade striped cotton bags to carry all the groceries home. I would have gone too, if I hadn't been in disgrace.

Dad was probably at church, at some meeting or other.

I was all alone. And I was really, really sick. I half fell, half climbed down the ladder from the loft and collapsed on my bed. I called out, but nobody was there. The room was spinning, my head was pounding, and I felt like throwing up.

Why hadn't I remembered this before? Why was I remembering it now?

Rose

"Dad!" I said sharply. "Do you understand what I'm saying?"

"No!" he said again, closing his eyes. He clutched his head and bent forward, as if he could block me out.

"DAD!"

He raised his head. His eyes were full of tears.

"Kendrick told me—" he said in a broken voice. "I didn't want to believe her. She said you were—acting strangely. Seeing things. I can't bear it, Rosie, not again. Tell me it isn't true."

If only I could.

"It is true, Dad. I see ghosts. I see them all the time. I've seen them all my life."

He crumpled.

"No," he said, burying his head in his arms and curling into a ball. "I can't lose you too. No."

I felt the ground dropping away beneath me. What had happened to my big strong father who never raised his voice and always kept his head? What had I done?

WHISPERING

Polly

The room was dim. I got up to switch on the overhead light, but it didn't work. Neither did the lamp in the corner. A power outage, maybe.

But the circle of light under the streetlight was still there outside the window. Where was Rose? And where was my family? They should have been home by now.

I felt very, very tired, and my head still hurt. I sank back into the chair and closed my eyes and went back to that day. The eggs day.

I remembered lying on my bed for a long, long time. And nobody came.

All I could think about was the pounding in my head. I kept thinking I couldn't stand it for one more minute, but it kept on. Then I started to hear whispering in the walls, voices swirling around me, like a radio was on. I opened my eyes, but the room was empty, filled with white, burning light. The sun, shining in the window. I shut them again. I was floating, floating on a hard, bright sea, up and down, up and down.

Then the twins came.

Rose

I glanced past my father at Winnie, who was still standing behind his chair, her eyes fixed on him. She didn't move or look at me.

Suddenly I was angry. Why was I doing this? Risking everything. Nothing but trouble was going to come of it. My father was collapsing into a little boy. I couldn't help him. He was supposed to help me! That's what fathers were supposed to do. This was all wrong. He was a mess.

"Dad!" I almost shouted at him. "Stop it! Sit up and listen to me. Why didn't you tell me you had a sister? Why didn't you tell me she died? Why didn't you tell me anything?"

My father looked up, gripping the edge of the desk with both hands. His face was white.

"Nobody knows," he whispered. "Not even your mother."

He didn't look like my father anymore. He was the little boy on the bridge, eyes big with horror.

I persisted. "Why? How could you keep that a secret?"

He looked up at me.

"It was my fault she died. It was all my fault."

NONSENSE

Polly

I remembered hearing the twins whispering at my door. I'd tried to sit up, but my head was so heavy on the pillow I couldn't raise it.

"Tell Mum," I croaked. "I'm sick."

"You're not sick," said Mark, coming over to the bed and looking down at me. "You're pretending."

"No, I'm really sick. Tell Mum," and then I sank back down into the white, white waves.

A long time later I heard Mum come in. She plonked Susie down in her crib for a nap and talked to her for a minute, rubbing her back the way she always did to get her to go to sleep.

I couldn't open my eyes because the light was too bright. I tried to call out to her but I couldn't get the word out.

"Polly," she said. "The boys tell me you're pretending to be sick. That's very childish. You can come down and join the family for lunch whenever you're ready."

She left.

Rose

Winnie knelt down beside my father and put her hand on his arm.

"Willie, it was an accident. You've got to believe me. It wasn't your fault."

He just kept staring into space. He didn't hear her.

"Dad," I said loudly. "She's sorry. She says it was an accident."

Then his eyes focused on me, and suddenly the spell we were under broke with a snap and he was Dad again.

"Rosie, we shouldn't be talking about this. It happened a long time ago. It's over. I don't know how you found out about Winnie, but you need to put this out of your mind. It's not healthy. I'll take you to a psychiatrist. I'll get you help."

"Dad, you've got to listen to me. Winnie is right beside you. I can see her as plain as day. She needs you to listen to me."

"No!" he yelled, pounding on the desk and standing up. "I will not allow you to go the way Winnie went. I will not allow it!"

"It's no use," I said to Winnie. "He won't listen. I told you what would happen. He thinks I'm crazy, just like I knew he would."

Winnie whipped around the desk and lunged towards me, her face dark, her eyes flashing, the black of her dress and hair starting to swirl into the form of the Door Jumper. "You have to make him understand," she said, looming over me. "You have to!"

I stood my ground. "I'm telling you, he won't listen to me! He doesn't listen to me any more than he listens to you! He

235

doesn't hear me and he doesn't see me. He never has. I'm invisible, just like you."

Winnie began to spin like a top—or a tornado—and the room started to fill up with her black rage. I took a step back, but my father still didn't see her or feel her. He rushed across the room, grabbed me by the shoulders and gave me a shake.

"Rosie!" he shouted. "Stop talking to ghosts. Talk to me! What do you mean, you're invisible? I see you. Of course I see you."

That did it. With two of them attacking me I finally snapped. I didn't care anymore if he thought I was nuts or if Winnie blew the house down. I shook off his grip and stamped my foot.

"NO YOU DON'T!" I bellowed.

My father blinked in surprise. He'd never heard me make that much noise before. The raging cloud that was Winnie hung suspended in the air for a moment, halted by the force of my voice.

I stamped my foot again. "You don't talk to me for weeks. Neither does Mother. I never know when you'll be home or away. I thought you were in Montreal, and then I see you walking down the street! You never tell me what's happening. You never tell me anything! You leave me alone all the time. Nobody talks to me. The teachers at school, the kids—I feel invisible all the time. I'm always by myself with nobody but ghosts."

"Rosie, that's not true—" he began in a softer voice, trying to calm me down.

"Tell me this! Tell me this one thing," I shouted. "Tell me if I'm dead. I feel dead. There is no evidence that I'm not dead. Did I die last summer? When I was in the hospital? Did I die? Did I?"

"Of course you didn't die, Rose. What absolute nonsense!" said a voice behind me.

My mother stood in the doorway, still in her coat, hat and gloves. Winnie was gone. A waft of Chanel #5 perfume drifted into the room.

"What on earth is going on?" she asked, looking over my head at my father. "First you disappear from the office, leaving no word with anyone. Then I get a very strange phone call from the library about Rose."

Uh-oh.

MOTHERS

Polly

Here's the thing. I used to pretend I was sick sometimes. When I was younger. Well, up to last year. You see, when I was sick, I got to stay home from school, read books all day in bed, and Mum brought me glasses of orange juice and even ginger ale sometimes. I'd get her all to myself. She kept a box of "sick toys" in a cupboard in her room, and we were only allowed to play with them when we were sick. When I was little, I got pretty excited about those painted wooden blocks, puzzles and special books.

So sometimes, if I didn't feel like facing school, I'd pretend I was sick. It worked okay, as long as I didn't do it too often. But Mum started catching on, and it got harder and harder to convince her, and then she kept telling me the story about the boy who cried "Wolf!" and how dangerous it was to lie all the time.

I hadn't pretended to be sick for months. But they hadn't forgotten.

Rose

My father went over to my mother.

"Mary, I'm sorry. I— Something came up. I had to leave . . .
I need to talk to you." He glanced over at me. It was obvious
he didn't want to say more in front of me.

My mother took charge, the way she always did, as if we
were difficult employees who needed handling.

"Well, that's fine, William, we can certainly talk about it.
But first I need to hear about this nonsense with Rose. Just let
me get my coat off."

As she disappeared into the hall, Father whispered to me,
"Don't mention Winnie!"

He looked just like one of Polly's little brothers when he
said it. What was wrong with him?

Mother came bustling back into the room, swept my cloak
off my shoulders and guided me over to a footstool by the fire.

"Let's all just sit down quietly and discuss this rationally."

She sat down calmly in my grandfather's big armchair and
smoothed her skirts. My father pulled the desk chair over and
sat on it. They towered over me.

"Now, Rose," she began, fixing me with a cool look.
"What's all this about being dead?"

MENINGITIS

Polly

The day I was sick, I lay on my bed all afternoon, drifting in and out, up and down, my head pounding. When my mother came in to get Susie up for her nap she sat on the edge of my bed.

"Polly, are you really sick?" she asked. "Or are you still sulking?"

"My head hurts," I said.

She laid a cool hand on my forehead.

"You are rather feverish," she said. "Let me get you some aspirin."

She helped me drink some water and take the aspirin.

"Maybe it's flu," she said. "Let's get you into your PJs."

She helped me get undressed and into my soft flannel pajamas, then pulled back the sheets so I could get into bed. Then she took Susie downstairs and I was alone again.

The sheets felt cool at first. But the room turned round and round, like I was on a merry-go-round. I closed my eyes, but I could still feel it spinning. Round and round, up and down.

I must have gone to sleep. When I woke up it was very dark. My neck felt stiff. I was itchy, and the walls were still whispering at me.

"Mum?" I called out, but I couldn't make a noise loud enough for anyone to hear. There was another noise that was drowning it out. The pounding of my head. A drum. Why didn't everyone in the house hear it? It went on and on. Thumping.

Somehow I got myself out of bed and crawled through the hall to the stairs. I went down them on my bum, one at a time. I stopped a couple of times and called for my mother, but my voice was still too weak for anyone to hear. The stairs spun round and round.

I crawled around the corner to my parents' bedroom and pulled myself up by the door handle so I was standing in the open doorway and called out one more time.

"MUM!"

There was a murmur from the bed, and the covers heaved up and suddenly the room was filled with a flash of burning white light.

"Mum!" I cried, again, the drum pounding in my ears. "Mum, I think I'm dying."

Rose

Sitting on the footstool, I felt like I was two again, a very small person. My heart was thumping. I knew I was going to sound ridiculous. To make it worse, Winnie had reappeared (in human form rather than a tempest) and was standing behind my mother, staring at my father with that hungry look.

"In the summer," I began, "when I was so sick—"

"When you had meningitis," said my mother.

"Is that what it was?" I asked.

"Yes, you know it was," she answered. "We told you, Dr. Wolf told you, many times, in the hospital. Meningitis."

"Dr. Wolf?" I said. "Is that really his name?"

"Yes, of course it's his name. Don't be silly, Rose."

"I don't remember," I said. "I don't remember anybody telling me. All I remember is the headache, and my neck hurt, and throwing up. And the Wolf Doctor—"

"Dr. Wolf, not the Wolf Doctor," interrupted my mother.

My father looked sorrowfully at me, and Winnie laughed.

"Dr. Wolf," I said. "Dr. Wolf saying I should go to the hospital and you crying and then everything was so white and cold."

"You were very, very sick," said my mother, her mouth tightening into a thin line. "It was an epidemic. Children all over the city were coming down with it, and many of them died. But you didn't. You got better. What on earth would make you say you were dead, Rose?"

"Because I feel dead! I feel all drifty and foggy and invisible. Nobody ever talks to me at school. It's like they don't see me. You and Father are never home. You don't talk to me! I can go for days and days and no one speaks one word to me. Not even Kendrick."

It felt good to finally say it out loud. I felt something unlocking inside my throat.

My parents exchanged pained looks.

"Rosie," said my father. "That can't be true. You must be exaggerating. We talk to you. We have breakfast with you nearly every morning."

"BUT NOBODY SAYS ANYTHING!" I said, jumping to my feet. "You read the newspaper and ask me to pass the marmalade, that's all! Even the Breakfast Ghost pays more attention to me than you do. At least he sees me."

"Breakfast Ghost?" said my mother, frowning. "Rose, you are letting your imagination get out of hand. Of course we speak to you. I speak to you every day."

"But we don't talk! You don't tell me anything! And I heard you crying one night, Mother, crying about losing me. Saying your baby was dead. What am I supposed to think?"

My mother's hand flew to her mouth. "What do you know about the baby?" she whispered, then turned to my father. "William, did you—?"

He shook his head.

"What baby?" I asked.

EVERYTHING HURTS

Polly

I don't remember a lot after that. Voices, arms lifting me up. An ambulance siren and then the hospital. Everything hurt in the hospital. The lights were unbearably bright, the sheets were white and hard, they kept sticking needles into me and then . . . then . . . then everything began to fade. All I could feel was rocking, and all I could see was white, and there was nothing but white everywhere, and I couldn't see my hands and I couldn't hear anything and I couldn't see my mother and—

I sat up with a start. I was still sitting in the dark living room. Outside, the white circle of the streetlight was still empty. No Rose.

My head still hurt, but it was a faint, whispering headache, not a bad one. Funny that I'd forgotten all that stuff about being sick and being in the hospital. It must have been after I got better and came home that I fell asleep in the loft, and the twins were looking for me, and I went up to the attic and met Rose. Weird. I'd have to tell her about it and see what she thought. Maybe that bad headache and whatever I had made me lose my memory.

Rose had to be home by now. I let myself out the front door and went silently down the steps. When I entered the circle of light on the sidewalk, the one I'd been staring at for so long, I stopped for a moment and looked up at my sitting room window. It was still dark, but for a moment I thought I saw the figure of someone sitting in the chair, looking out at me. Probably just a shadow, but for a second or two I thought I was seeing myself, looking out at myself. A little shiver went down my spine.

The porch light was on at Rose's house, and a faint light glowed from the hall, but their living room was dark.

I'd lost my nerve about ringing the bell. Her parents might be home by now. I walked up the dark path beside their house on the cemetery side and opened the gate to the backyard.

The path was lined with uneven paving stones, and I had to walk slowly in the shadows, feeling my way carefully. On my left the ground fell off steeply, and then the hill in the cemetery reared up, gravestones silhouetted against the dark sky. I rounded the corner and slipped behind some bushes so I could look into the back of the house without being seen.

Light poured out from the French doors that led to—to Rose's father's study, I guessed. I'd never been in there. I could see bookcases lining the walls, a big desk and . . . people. They were there. Rose, her father, her mother—and Winnie.

I took a couple of steps closer, taking care not to step inside the light. It was strange, watching them through the window, as if it were a movie. The glass must have been dirty because I couldn't see through it really clearly. It seemed to ripple a bit. Their voices were muffled, so I had no idea what they were saying.

Rose's mother was pretty, but she didn't look at all like Rose. She was normal-sized, not tiny, and her hair was blond, softly curled around her face. She looked very tired.

I couldn't see her father very clearly, mostly just his back. He looked tall too, with broad shoulders, but his hair looked like Rose's—dark and thick and curly.

Winnie stood behind Rose's mother, staring at Rose's father. She looked different from the wild, angry girl I'd glimpsed in Rose's attic. She looked sad—and longing. Like she wanted something so badly but didn't know how to get it.

I moved a bit to the left so I could see Rose, who was partially blocked by her father. Her expression made me catch my breath. She looked angrier than I had ever seen her. I think she was shouting. She looked—like Winnie. And Winnie looked like Rose.

I turned my head from one to the other. Both dressed in black. Both with white faces. I started to wonder if I had been wrong, and it was Rose who was staring longingly at her father and Winnie standing in front of the fire, shouting at them. Which was which? And which was the ghost? Or were they both ghosts?

Rose

My mother smoothed her skirt and exchanged looks with my father.

"It happened last winter," she said, trying to gain control of her voice, which wobbled. Not something I often heard from my mother. She cleared her throat. "I was—pregnant. Only a few months. We didn't tell you because—well, there were complications, and we weren't sure the baby was going to make it. And—she didn't. She died."

Her voice started wobbling again.

"She?" I said. It came out as a raspy croak.

"Yes," said my mother. Her eyes filled with tears. "A sister. You would have had a sister. I was five months pregnant when I lost her."

"Five months? And you didn't tell me?"

"It was always a risky pregnancy. We didn't tell anyone, except my parents."

She fumbled in her purse for a handkerchief and wiped her eyes.

"Is that why you were in the hospital? Is that why you've been so sad all this time?"

She nodded, unable to speak. My father went to her and put his arm around her shoulders.

"Mary," he said. "Don't."

"Why didn't you tell me?" I cried. "You always treat me like I'm not here! Like I'm not important! I have a right to know what's happening."

"We talked about telling you," said my father. "But—well—your grandmother died not long after, and we decided it was all a bit too much for you to take in."

I felt the anger rising up again inside me: a hot red wave.

"You don't *know* what I can take," I said through gritted teeth, trying to hold the wave back. "You don't *know* what I have to live with every day."

My father started looking nervous again. I knew he was afraid I was going to start talking about Winnie and ghosts.

"We made the decision not to tell you," said my mother, rallying. "Perhaps we were wrong. It's been a difficult year, Rose, for everybody. There have been a number of grown-up things going on between your father and me, and the business, that you can't possibly understand. We have tried to protect you from that."

I opened my mouth and the wave swept out.

"I understand this," I said. "You don't love me. You don't see me. You don't want to see what's going on inside me. You're afraid of me. You think there's something wrong with me and if you just keep ignoring me it will go away."

"No, Rosie, that's not true," protested my father.

"Don't call me Rosie!" I yelled at him. "That's a baby name. I'm not a baby."

"You are certainly acting like a baby," said my mother sharply. "A baby having a temper tantrum."

WE LOST HER

Polly

"Polly!" whispered a voice out of the darkness.

I jumped and gave a little yelp.

Mark and Matthew materialized beside me.

"What are you doing here?" I whispered back. "You nearly scared me to death."

"We don't want you going near the Ghost Girl," said Matthew, pulling at my sleeve.

"Come home," said Mark, pulling at my other sleeve. "Come back to the attic where you're safe."

"Not this again," I said, shaking them off. "What's with you two? Rose is my friend. If you want to see a real Ghost Girl," I said, pushing Mark in front of me, "look in there. Can you see her?"

"Who?" he said.

"Winnie." I pointed to the one with the old-fashioned white collar. That had to be Winnie, no matter what the expression on her face. "She's standing behind Rose's mum. She looks just like Rose, but she's a ghost. A real ghost."

The boys stood in front of me, staring into the room.

"That's the Ghost Girl," breathed Mark. I could feel him beginning to tremble. "That's the one we've been seeing, the one in the window. The one that's after you, Polly."

"The one that wants to steal your soul," said Matthew.

"Well, that's Winnie, not Rose. Rose is my friend, and she's the one you've been seeing and calling the Ghost Girl. She's over there, in front of the fire." I pointed my finger.

"Two Ghost Girls?" said Matthew. "There's two of them? Twins?"

Suddenly the door behind Winnie started to open, and she ducked out of sight. A shadowy figure stood at the door, holding it open and saying something, then someone else walked into the room.

"What's Mum doing there?" said Matthew.

Rose

Winnie smirked at me over my mother's shoulder. She was enjoying this.

Before I could respond to my mother, the door opened and Kendrick stood there.

"Mrs. Lacey from next door wants a word," she said, giving me a pointed look. As if she knew I was about to get into big trouble.

Polly's mother walked in. She looked much as she had earlier that day—she was still wearing the red coat and her glasses were slipping off her nose. But she looked upset, almost as if she had been crying.

"I'm so sorry to intrude," she said, looking at my mother, "but something rather upsetting has come to my attention, and I think I should clear it up right now before it goes any further."

My mother and father had both got to their feet as she came in.

"Is it about the library?" said my mother quickly. "I had a phone call today from Mrs. Gardner. Something about an over-due book, and some silliness with the children."

Mrs. Lacey swallowed. "Yes, but it's gone a bit beyond silly, I'm afraid. Can I speak to you alone, please?" she continued, deliberately not looking at me.

My mother pulled her businesswoman attitude round her like a cloak.

"If it's something to do with my daughter, Mrs.—Mrs. Lacey, is it?"

Polly's mother nodded.

"I think we should get it out in the open, and I'm sure Rose can help us straighten it out."

"Well . . ." said Mrs. Lacey looking from my mother to me. "If you think it's best."

My mother nodded. Mrs. Lacey stood up a little straighter and continued.

"At first I thought it was some game the twins were playing with your daughter. I know they tease her. But I've spoken to them, and they swear they don't know anything about the book. They're very mischievous but they don't lie, as a rule. Somehow your daughter got that library book from inside our house. And that's not all."

Mrs. Lacey held up the striped shopping bag.

"This afternoon I found your daughter hiding this. It's one of my shopping bags. I made them myself, so there's no mistaking it. I'd like to know where she got it. And there have been other things. Missing food. Missing cake, missing cookies. Things being moved around. I've been accusing the twins, but now, with this book—well, I think somehow your daughter has been coming into my house and taking things."

She looked at me, a little breathless. My parents' mouths had dropped open.

"Are you accusing my daughter of stealing?" said my mother in her very quiet, you're-about-to-be-fired-so-be-very-very-careful tone of voice.

"I don't like to," said Mrs. Lacey. "She seems a very . . . very . . . well . . . nice girl," she said a bit uncertainly, glancing at my wild hair. "But I don't know what other explanation there could possibly be. And as I'm sure you understand, the book is particularly upsetting, because it was one my daughter took out of the library, before she—"

Here Mrs. Lacey stopped and took a deep breath. She seemed to be struggling with tears.

"Before—before she died," she went on with an effort. "And we've had a couple of notices from the library, but we've never been able to find it."

I had been waiting to get a chance to speak and tell them to just ask Polly and she'd explain everything, but something started ringing in my ears and I couldn't say a word. Everything in the room slowed and I felt like I was underwater. The grown-ups' voices were coming from far, far away.

"Your daughter?" said my mother, her briskness falling away. "I'm very sorry, I didn't know. You say the book was your daughter's? You had a daughter who—died?"

Mrs. Lacey nodded dumbly, and her eyes overflowed again.

"I'm sorry," she gasped, putting out her arm to my mother, as if she were going to fall over. "This book business has brought it all back. You think you're past the worst and then it just—it just—"

My mother was at her side in an instant, guiding her to the chair, sitting her down.

"Can I get you anything?" offered my father. "Some water?"

Mrs. Lacey shook her head and tried to smile through her tears. The smile made her look even more like Polly.

"No, I'll be all right in a minute. It was all very sudden, you see. Last spring. The meningitis epidemic. We lost her. Polly. I thought you knew."

COLD

Polly

Everyone was on their feet now and I couldn't see their faces. Rose was hidden behind her dad. Winnie was nowhere to be seen. The twins and I stood rooted to the spot, as if we were watching a movie. There was a flurry, and people moved, and Mr. and Mrs. McPherson were bending over someone in the chair, and Rose was standing like a statue in front of the fire, her face white. She moved slowly past them and out the door, as if she were sleepwalking. Then the person in the chair got up. It was Mum, and she was clutching a handkerchief to her face, and Mrs. McPherson had her arm around her shoulder and was leading her from the room.

"Mum," said Mark in a broken voice.

"See, now she's upset again," said Matthew. "It's all your fault, Polly."

"My fault? What did I do?"

"Nothing," said Mark. "Shut up, Matt."

"Well, it is her fault. If she hadn't—Hey!" Mark pushed him over.

"If I hadn't what?"

"It doesn't matter," said Matt. "Let's go home."

For the first time, I realized I had come out without my coat. I was very, very cold.

Rose

The world spun around me. Everything was dropping away. I felt sick, like I was going to throw up. In a blur I saw my parents bending over Polly's mum. Winnie stood on the far side of the room, watching me with a strange expression on her face.

I felt completely detached from all of them, as if they were on television and I could turn them all off by walking away. I felt more like a ghost than ever.

I walked past them all and out the door. Nobody saw me go.

The hall was dark, full of shadows. A haunted house, Polly said.

I picked up the box from the hall table and slowly walked up the stairs. Each stair could have been a mountain—it was hard to lift my feet, as if they were weighed down by bricks. I felt dizzy, as if the staircase and the walls and the furniture in the house and my parents and Mrs. Lacey had all been thrown up into the air and were spinning madly around. Nothing was solid, except my heavy feet and the thick pain in my throat, like I'd swallowed something too big and it was caught there, making it difficult to breathe.

I moved through my grandmother's room, where the faint smell of roses whispered to me. The rug with the flowers seemed to stretch on forever. I finally made it into the closet and climbed up the endless ladder to the attic. The house still spun around me, like a spinning top, with all the colors whirling together, around and around.

I put the box on the floor and pulled myself up into the old stuffed chair in the dark. I took a careful breath. Something fluttered in my throat.

Polly. Polly was the ghost, not me.

PART FIVE

THE SWALLOW

O Swallow, Swallow, flying, flying South,
Fly to her, and fall upon her gilded eaves,
And tell her, tell her, what I tell to thee.

ALFRED, LORD TENNYSON, "O SWALLOW, SWALLOW"

UNDERWATER

Polly

I looked back into the study. The glass was even more ripply now, and it was a lot harder to see in. But I could just make out Mr. McPherson, sitting in the chair, staring into the fire. He buried his face in his hands.

"Come back with us, Polly," said Mark, tugging at my sleeve again.

I shook my head. I felt as if I were deep underwater, and everything was thick and slow. I didn't want to move or think. I just wanted to keep watching what was happening in that study, like I was watching a show on TV and needed to know how it turned out.

Winnie appeared again, behind Mr. McPherson. She stretched out her hand and softly stroked his hair. It looked like she was saying something, but I couldn't hear. He didn't move for a minute. Then he raised his head.

He was crying. I'd never seen a man cry before. His face was collapsed on itself. He rubbed his eyes like a little boy.

Winnie knelt by his side and stroked his arm, looking up into his face and speaking to him.

It was obvious that he didn't see her. But somehow, I felt he knew she was there. It made me feel good. Rose must have given him the message, and now they could say good-bye.

Rose

How was it possible? I'd hugged her, I'd felt her warm hand on mine, I'd seen her devouring shortbread, I'd heard her laughing. How could Polly be dead?

But then I remembered the sight of her pale white hand on the floor of the attic after Winnie attacked her, and her pale face, and Winnie screaming at me, "She's dead!"

The very first time I met her, when I heard her voice in the attic, I did think she was a ghost. An invisible ghost who was trying to trick me. But she had also tricked herself, because there was no way Polly knew she was dead. She was going to school, eating dinner, talking to her brothers and sisters. But were they talking back?

I tried to think, sitting there in the dark with my world spinning out of control, tried to remember if I had ever seen anyone talking to Polly. Mrs. Gardner at the library? No, she had just yelled at the twins and ignored Polly and me when we were there. The kids at her school? No, Polly had walked behind them, all by herself. The twins? I'd never seen Polly and the twins together, but they always talked about her to me as if she were alive.

Or did they? What if they could see ghosts, the way I could? That would explain why they were so worried about me spending time with Polly. They thought I was a ghost, and they were afraid I would tell her she was dead, and then she would disappear.

It was true. Polly was dead.

I couldn't bear it. I felt a scream of "NO!" rising inside me, but nothing could come past the huge lump stopping up my throat.

I slipped off the chair to the floor and curled into a ball. Everything hurt, but my throat worst of all. It felt as if a bird were trapped in there, struggling to get out, and every time it flapped its wings they scraped against the inside of my throat, cutting me.

A swallow.

I could feel the scratch of the dusty floorboards against my cheek. The pain was beating inside me like a pulse. Not Polly. Not her. It should have been me who was a ghost.

Finally, finally, the swallow wrenched its way out, tearing at my throat, and I began to cry—huge, jerky sobs that sounded like they came from someone else.

NO REPLY

Polly

"Come on," said Matthew. "Back to the attic. You'll be safe there, Polly."

I let them pull me along the path and onto the street, then up the stairs and into our house. I could hear faint noises from the kitchen—voices—but they sounded very far away. I walked up the stairs, Mark in front and Matthew behind, as if I were their captive. I was feeling very tired, and with every step my feet felt heavier than the step before, but I let them lead me to my closet.

"Go on," said Mark. "Go up."

I could see the edge of Susie's crib through the doorway. I could see my bed and the bookshelf above it with my old dolls sitting in a row. The boys looked up at me, worried.

"You'll be okay," said Matthew. "Have a nap, and when you wake up everything will be back to normal, just like before."

"Okay," I said, "I'll do that."

They looked uncertainly at me, but I turned away and climbed up into my loft, then pushed open the trapdoor and heaved myself into the attic.

It was dark. I crawled over to the wall and burrowed under the blankets.

Rose

I lay on the floor in the dark. It could have been a few minutes or a few hours. Eventually I stopped crying and the world stopped spinning. The house and the people in it slowly dropped down to the ground. I sat up.

I tried to call her. "Polly." It came out as a faint whisper.

I tried again. "Polly." A little louder. "Polly, come back."

There was no reply.

My voice was too faint. She probably couldn't hear it through the wall. I stood up, picked up the flashlight from beside my chair and pushed through the boxes to the hidden door.

It was dark and narrow. I remembered the last time I had come through the passage, after the walls of Polly's attic had closed in on me, how narrow and airless it had felt, how I swore I would never go back.

I bent down and crawled in. If anything, it was worse than before. It seemed smaller, and I dragged myself along, picking up splinters on my elbows and knees. I went as fast as I could and burst through the door at Polly's end, taking deep breaths of the stale attic air.

I flashed the light around. It was empty, except for the pile of blankets by the wall.

"Polly?" I whispered. I expected the blankets to heave up at any minute and reveal her, tousled from sleep perhaps, grinning at me, glasses askew.

The blankets didn't move. But the lump in the middle was just the shape it would be if a girl Polly's size was curled up underneath.

I walked over and poked it gently.

"Polly?"

I poked a little harder. The lump collapsed beneath my hand. I pulled the blankets back but there was nothing there—

Except a lingering warmth, as if someone had just left.

I sat down among the blankets, stunned. She was gone. She was really gone.

TWINS

Rose

I put my head in my hands. The swallow fluttered in my chest now, beating sharply against my ribs, and the world began to spin again.

A long time later it stopped. I heard a scrambling from the other end of the attic. Mice? I groped for the flashlight.

The bar of light revealed a small, scared face full of freckles, sticking up through the trapdoor. One of the Horrors. I didn't know which.

"Polly?" said the boy, shielding his eyes against the light in his face.

"No, it's Rose," I replied, my voice a hoarse whisper. He ducked back down out of sight for a consultation with his brother.

"Oh, come on up," I said. "I won't bite you."

Slowly the head came back up, followed by the rest of him, and then the other one. They huddled together at the opposite end of the attic.

"Where's Polly?" said the first one. "What have you done with her?"

"I didn't do anything. But she's gone," I answered.

Whispers again.

"We know you're twins," said the first one. "We saw the two of you through the window."

"What window?"

"Your house," said the other one. "A while ago. Polly was with us. And we saw Mum come in and start crying. And then Polly started acting really weird, and we brought her back here to keep her safe. Where is she?"

I shook my head. "I don't know."

Silence. Then the first one said, with a tremble in his voice, "We know you're the Ghost Girl."

"You want to steal her soul," said the other.

"No," I said, shaking my head. "I'm not the Ghost Girl. That's Winnie. She looks like me . . . but she's not me. I didn't want to hurt Polly."

They inched closer, and I handed the first one the flashlight.

"Look at me," I said. "I'm not dead."

They held the light on me for a long time.

"You look like a ghost," said the first one finally.

"But I'm not. I was Polly's friend. You don't have to be scared of me."

They looked at each other. Some kind of communication was going on between them. Whatever it was, they seemed to come to an agreement.

"Okay," said the first one. "Maybe you're not a ghost."

"But if you're not a ghost," said the other one, "then how did you get into our attic?"

I grinned at them. "Secret passage," I said.

"wow!" they breathed in unison.

I reached over and took the flashlight back, shining it into their pale faces.

"Which of you is which?"

"I'm Mark," said the first one.

"I'm Matthew," said the second.

"Okay. So you guys can see ghosts, right? How long have you been able to see them?"

Mark shrugged. "Not that long."

"Just since Polly—Polly—" said Matthew.

"Since Polly got sick and died," whispered Mark. "We thought it was our fault. We told Mum she was pretending, but she wasn't, she was really sick, and then the next day she . . . she . . . died in the hospital, and we thought it was our fault. Then at the funeral we started to see ghosts in the cemetery, and when we got home Polly was in her room, reading, just like usual."

"But nobody else could see her," said Matthew. "Just us. So we played along with her. She didn't know she was dead. We thought we could keep her."

"She wasn't always there," said Mark. "She came and went, and she didn't seem to understand that days and weeks were passing. She was all mixed up. But she thought everything was normal. She went to school, she did her homework, ate dinner. And she never seemed to notice that no one was talking to her except us."

"How did she eat dinner? I mean, there wasn't a place set for her or food or a chair, was there?"

The boys looked at each other and shrugged.

"She just would appear at the table, like normal, eating," said Mark. "She'd have a plate of food just like she was alive, and she'd eat away and listen to the conversation and laugh and talk and somehow . . ."

"And somehow she never realized," continued Matthew. "Like she was in a bubble. But then we started seeing the Ghost Girl around your house."

"And she was really scary, like the one in the book," said Mark.

"And we knew she was going to tell Polly that she was dead and steal her soul away, and then Polly would go."

"But was the Ghost Girl me or the other one?" I asked.

They exchanged glances.

"We can't tell the difference. We thought there was only one."

A muffled voice came from a long, long way below.

"Mark! Matthew!"

They jumped.

"It's Dad," said Mark.

"We gotta go," said Matthew. They popped down through the trapdoor and drew it shut behind them.

I sat there for a while, thinking about what they had said. A bubble. She was living in a bubble, where she was still alive. She wasn't ready to die, so she stayed. And found me.

I shook my head. I still couldn't believe it. How was she a ghost, and I didn't recognize it? She seemed so alive. How was she warm? How did she eat? How did she . . . breathe? After Winnie had tried to kill her in my attic I'd breathed life into her. I could feel it. I felt her heart beating under her skin.

What was it that made her a ghost? What was it that made her dead? Just . . . believing it?

I shook my head. No. There had to be more to it than that.

I took one last look around her attic. She wasn't there anymore.

"Good-bye, Polly," I whispered and crawled back through the passage, and home.

OLD ENOUGH

Rose

Mother came up later to see if I wanted any supper. I didn't.

She sat on the edge of my bed. I had been crying again, and I lay curled up with my back to her, so she couldn't see my face.

"Rose," she said.

"I didn't steal that stuff," I mumbled. "I didn't go in their house."

"I know," she said. "Don't worry about that now. It's some misunderstanding. Mrs. Lacey is very upset. Poor thing. Your father and I—" She stopped, swallowed, and then started again. "She told us what happened. It was just the same as with you. Meningitis. Only—only they didn't catch it in time and their girl died. Very sad. Her little boys have had trouble accepting it, she says. They keep playing games as if their sister were alive. They've been playing tricks, and they must have slipped that book into your schoolbag, or something like that. It's all over, Rose, you don't need to worry about it." She fell silent for a moment.

"About the baby," she finally said, softly.

I turned over and looked at her. She had both hands on her lap and was fiddling with her wedding ring. She looked over at me.

"You're right. We should have told you."

"Yes," I said. "I knew something was wrong and it worried me, Mother. I didn't know why you were so sad."

She took a deep breath. "We realized we needed to leave my parents' house and be on our own. Your father hasn't been happy at work, and he's thinking about going back to teaching. Your grandfather doesn't understand, and—well, we needed to get away. Losing the baby, and Granny McPherson . . . it's been difficult." Her voice broke.

I reached out and touched her arm.

"Mother," was all I could say.

She smiled, shaking her head, and the tears spilled out of her eyes.

"We thought we were going to lose you too," she said. "Last summer, when you were so sick. You could so easily have gone, like that little girl next door. Poor Mrs. Lacey."

She produced a clean handkerchief from her suit pocket and wiped her eyes. She looked up at me again.

"Rose, we do love you. Very much. I don't suppose we show you enough. I'm so sorry that you've been so lonely, and so sad."

I crept forward and she put her arms around me. We sat like that for a long time, with the house very still and quiet around us.

THE PURPLE SHAWL

Rose

When I woke up on Saturday morning, I thought I was sick. All my limbs felt heavy and I could barely sit up. The house was quiet. A dull gray light filtered in through the curtains, and when I pulled them back I saw the sky was filled with a thick blanket of clouds.

Every step I took felt like an effort, and my throat was tight, as if I was about to start crying again. I hauled myself across the hall, into my grandmother's room, and stood at the closet door looking at the ladder that led to the attic. What was the point? Polly wasn't up there.

But I went up anyway, one rung at a time. I wondered if I had caught some kind of flu. My head throbbed. I crawled across the floor and leaned against the chair, without even the strength to lift myself into it.

Polly. The weight in my chest shifted, and I began to cry again. It seemed like I had been crying all night, in my sleep, and here I was at it again.

Memories of Polly started jostling through my mind, one after another.

Polly as I had first seen her, in the cemetery, in her too-tight coat and her cat's-eye glasses. Polly running down the street after me, out of breath. Her expression whenever she got excited about ghosts. Stuffing her face full of cookies. Lying white and still on the attic floor after Winnie attacked her. Lying white and still.

I laid my face against the arm of the chair and closed my eyes.

"Come back," I whispered. "Please come back."

A hand gently stroked my hair. I turned my head.

It wasn't Polly. It was the old lady. She didn't have her knitting this time. She looked at me kindly and stroked my hair again.

"There, there," she said softly. "Such a lovely girl. There, there."

I let my head sink back against the chair and closed my eyes. She gave my back a little pat. Her hand was warm. It felt good to sit there feeling nothing for a while. After a long time, I sat up and turned to her again.

"What happened to your knitting?" I asked.

That wasn't what I'd meant to ask. I'd wanted to ask about Polly, how she could be a ghost and still breathe and eat, and why the old lady's hand was warm, and whether I would ever see Polly again, and a dozen other questions, but what came out of my mouth was the question about her knitting.

She smiled at me. I noticed then that she had blue eyes, like my mother's.

"I've finished," she said with some satisfaction. She reached down beside the chair and her hand came up full of soft, pale purple wool, all knitted into a shawl. She draped it around my shoulders.

"There you go, Rose," she said. "That will keep you warm."

I looked down at the delicate pattern, like rows of little scallop shells, and I drew it tight. It was light, but wonderfully warm.

"Thank you," I said, turning back to her.

The chair was empty.

TWO BREAKFASTS

Rose

I wore the shawl all weekend. All day over my clothes. All night over my pajamas. And when I went outside, I wore it as a big scarf, under my cloak.

My mother noticed it right away.

"Wherever did you get that, Rose?" she asked when I appeared in the kitchen Saturday morning, looking for breakfast.

"I . . . ummm . . . found it," I said. I still felt tired and heavy, but I was suddenly ravenous.

My mother gave me a searching look. "Go and sit down and I'll bring you some porridge."

Eww. Gooey porridge. Not exactly what I had in mind.

"Could— could I have bacon and eggs instead?" I asked. "And pancakes?"

Her eyes narrowed. "Whatever's got into you, Rose? You don't usually eat a big breakfast."

"I'm just . . . hungry," I replied. I didn't know myself what had got into me. One minute I was feeling like death warmed over and now suddenly I could eat two breakfasts.

Kendrick trekked in from the pantry and gave me the usual dirty look.

"Kendrick, would you be a dear and cook up some bacon and eggs for Rose? And some of your delicious buckwheat pancakes? She's woken up hungry."

Kendrick looked affronted but mumbled something, and my mother ushered me through the swinging door to the dining room.

She sat down beside me and took up the end of the shawl.

"I haven't seen this shawl for years," she mused. "Not since my mother packed it away when I was a girl. Where did you find it?"

"In—in—the attic," I said, dumbfounded.

"Well, however did it get there?" said my mother, stroking the soft wool. "My granny knit that shawl for me, before I was born. It was my baby shawl, and I always had it on my bed when I was little. But then it got packed away at some point and I never saw it again. I looked for it when you were a baby, but I couldn't find it. Fancy you coming across it, after all these years."

She sighed and put it down.

"My granny was a great knitter. She died when I was eight. I'm sure I've got a picture of her somewhere. I'll have to show you."

"Oh," was all I could say.

"She taught me to knit, when I was only six. I'd sit by her chair and she'd show me how to hold the needles, and how to wind the wool around. She was very patient, as I recall, because I kept forgetting how and she had to show me again and again." A smile played around my mother's lips, and she had a faraway look in her eyes. "You would have liked her, Rose. She was a very sweet old lady. No matter what was going on in our house, all the bustle and carry-on, Granny was always in her chair by the living room fire, knitting. I spent a lot of time just sitting with her."

My mother gave herself a shake.

"Enough of all that. I'm glad you have it now, however it turned up. On to business."

LEAVING SOCKS

Rose

My mother folded her hands together on the dining table and leaned towards me, much as if she were in a board meeting. She had that brisk air of organization that meant things were going to be accomplished quickly.

"Your father and I have been talking. He's decided to leave socks and go back to teaching. I support him completely, but it won't be easy. He has a lot of responsibilities at the company, and I'll have to find a replacement for him."

Kendrick chose that moment to bang through the door with the first part of my breakfast. I fell upon the eggs and toast while my mother watched me in silence for a moment.

"We're both concerned about you," she said finally.

I looked up at her, wondering if my father had mentioned anything about me seeing ghosts. It didn't seem likely, judging by the way he'd told me not to mention Winnie when my mother had stormed in last night. But you never knew with grown-ups.

My mother was frowning, but at least she didn't have that my-daughter's-so-weird expression on her face. Believe me, I knew that when I saw it.

"You spend too much time on your own, Rose," she said. "We'll have to do something about that. Once your father gets a job at a school, he'll be here to have supper with you every night. There's not much I can do about my schedule, but I can start taking Saturday afternoons off and perhaps we can have some family outings."

"I'd like that."

"And we agree with what you said about . . . telling you things. We need to communicate more with you. We forget you're not a little girl anymore." She stood up. "Your father and I need to go to work this morning. But we'll be home for a nice dinner together tonight."

Phew. My father couldn't have told her about the ghosts, or she would have brought it up by now.

As she came around the table on her way out the door, she stopped and fingered the shawl again.

"So strange that it should turn up again after all these years," she murmured and left.

DON'T TELL YOUR MOTHER

Rose

Well, that was my mother. Businesslike. Used to managing people. Now she was going to manage me. It was better than being overlooked, but I felt a stir of uneasiness. Family outings? I couldn't imagine it.

Kendrick stormed back in and plopped a plate of pancakes and a jug of maple syrup down on the table, snorted, and then returned to the kitchen.

I don't know where my appetite came from, but I plowed through those pancakes with no difficulty. I felt a prickle of guilt. It didn't seem right to be stuffing my face when I was so upset about Polly. And yet, the food made me feel better—more solid, less drifty. And surely Polly herself would approve? I gave a big sigh, got to my feet and wandered towards the window, which overlooked the back garden and the cemetery wall.

The heavy clouds lay over the day like a blanket of gloom. I could see the tips of some of the taller monuments beyond the stone wall, and the bare trees stood outlined against the sky.

The door behind me opened. I thought it was Kendrick, come to clear away the dishes, so I didn't turn around.

"Rose."

I turned. My father was standing just inside the door, looking at me.

"Oh," I said. "I thought you'd left."

"No, not quite. We'll be off in a minute. I wanted to . . . have a word . . . before we go."

I walked carefully to the table and sat down. He hesitated, then sat down kitty-corner from me. With an effort, I raised my eyes to look in his face, afraid of what I might see there.

The little boy was gone, thank goodness. But something had changed. He had dark shadows under his eyes, as if he hadn't slept much, but even so, his face looked lighter somehow. As if something had lifted.

"About . . . Winnie," he began, not looking me in the eye. "Your mother doesn't know. I will tell her . . . someday. Soon. Probably. But for now, let's just keep that between us."

I nodded.

"Did you really see her?"

I nodded again.

"Then you really see ghosts?" he went on, with an effort. "It's not . . . your imagination?"

I swallowed. "I really see them, Dad. It's scary."

He looked at me then. "I know. Winnie used to tell me about them. We talked a lot. We were close. She was good to me, Rosie. She never meant to hurt me." He shook his head. "After she died, our family was so quiet, with everyone in their own little world. My mother went a bit strange, I think, and my father—well, I don't think he ever forgave himself for trying to send Winnie away."

He sighed. "I wanted things to be different for you, Rosie. I wanted you to grow up in a happy house. But now it looks like I've made the same sort of family I came from, with things not talked about, and everyone keeping to themselves."

"I get lonely," I blurted out. "I miss you when you're away."

"I miss you too." He smiled at me. "That's going to change, Rose, when I go back to teaching. We're not going to leave you on your own so much."

He fell silent and started examining his fingernails for some reason. Then, as if he was gathering his courage, he looked up at me.

"About the ghosts . . . I think it's better if we don't tell your mother. I think she might . . . um . . . overreact."

"You believe me?" I said, my voice coming out sort of cracked, like I had laryngitis or something. "You don't think I should be locked up? Like Winnie?"

He shook his head. "No," he said. "You're not like Winnie. There was something dark and wild inside her that frightened everybody, including herself." He sighed. "It was all so long ago, Rose. But it cast a long shadow. I always thought it was all my fault, what happened that night." He passed his hand over his eyes.

"Winnie said it wasn't. She said it was an accident. She said she was sorry, Father, about everything. She wants you to be happy."

"Yes," he said softly. "Yes. I know." He looked back at me sadly.

"William!" called my mother from the hall. "Time to go!"

"I'll be right there, dear," he called out, getting to his feet. "Thank you for telling me, Rose, about Winnie, about the ghosts. We'll talk more later. Maybe I can help."

He came around the table and gave me a kiss good-bye. His fingers brushed against my shoulder.

"What a pretty shawl," he said. "So soft. Well, I must be on my way. Lots to do at the office. See you at supper," he said with a smile, and he left.

THE EMPTY CEMETERY

Rose

I turned back to the window and gazed out at the gray day. I felt like a huge weight was lifting off my shoulders. My father didn't think I was crazy. I could hardly believe it. I had told him I saw ghosts, and he had just . . . accepted it. How weird was that? And all because of Winnie, somehow.

And where was Winnie, anyway? I looked over my shoulder nervously. But the room was empty. Maybe she was right—maybe once my father had started to talk about her, and knew she was sorry, her spirit had been released. I wasn't sure. All I knew about was ghosts asking for help, not what happened if you helped them.

And Polly? What did she want? Had she been asking me for help, like all the other ghosts? My eyes went back to the cemetery. For the first time I could ever remember, I wanted to go there. I tightened the shawl around my shoulders and went looking for my cloak.

It was cold and damp outside. The kind of damp that creeps through your clothes, no matter how many layers you have on, and chills you to the bone. I walked quickly, trying to get warm.

The shawl felt soft against my chin, and I had a brief vision of the old lady—my great-grandmother—in the rocking chair when I was a baby, rocking and knitting.

There didn't seem to be anyone on the street. It was deserted. Lights gleamed faintly from some windows. It was a day to stay home, beside a fire if possible, with a good book. I huddled under my cloak and walked a bit faster.

When I turned on to Sumach Street, I walked beside the cemetery fence. This was unheard of for me. I peered through the iron railings, looking for signs of ghosts. But it was empty, except for the gravestones, and quiet.

I stopped at the gates and took a deep breath. "White light . . . white light," I whispered and then stopped. I didn't feel I needed that protection today. I wanted to see ghosts. One in particular. I walked through the wrought-iron gates, under the stone archway and into the Necropolis, the City of the Dead.

I wasn't sure which way to go. I didn't even know if Polly was buried here. But I thought she might come here. She'd said it was her favorite place.

I started towards the mausoleum. That took me around the little road, under the tall maple trees and down around the hill-side. There were no ghosts. At one point, as I turned the last corner, I thought I heard a whispering behind me, but when I turned there was nothing. The wind had picked up a bit—that must have been what I'd heard. I looked over my shoulder a few times but nothing moved. Only me.

I came to the steps of the mausoleum, where I had been the first time I saw Polly, and I sat down, drawing my cloak tight around me. I waited for a while, watching the bend in the road, half expecting to see her striding along with her hands in the pockets of her red coat and her hair flying around her face.

But she didn't come. Cold from the stone steps was seeping up through my cloak and turning me to ice. The shawl wasn't keeping me warm. There was no comfort anywhere: hard ground beneath me and all around me cold stone.

I got up and headed along the road, which led back up the hill in a roundabout fashion. I glanced over my shoulder. Still no ghosts. I walked slowly past the gravestones: some with tall angels, some with crosses, some with urns draped in shrouds. All gray and lonely and still.

"Polly," I whispered. "Polly, where are you?"

I found myself veering off the road in the direction of Winnie's grave. It wasn't hard to find, off in the corner by the fence. I stood looking down at it. I felt a faint stirring along the hairs on my arms as I saw my own name there. Winnifred Rose McPherson.

I turned to go back to the road, but my way was blocked. Winnie was standing there, watching me.

THE CHESHIRE CAT

Rose

Winnie was wearing a long black cloak, just like mine, and her hair was loose over her shoulders, just like mine. I had that dizzy feeling again, as if I were looking into a mirror.

"What?" I said hoarsely. "What do you want now? I did what you said."

She just looked at me.

"Isn't it okay with my father?" I asked. "Didn't he . . . forgive you? Or forgive himself? And now you can go?"

"You need to help her," said Winnie.

"Who? I need to help who?"

"Polly. Like you helped me. She needs you. That's why she came to you. That's why we all come to you. For help."

"But you don't understand," I said desperately. "I don't want to help ghosts. I don't want to see ghosts. I just want you to leave me alone. I just want to be normal."

Winnie laughed a nasty little laugh. "Don't kid yourself. You'll never be normal, Rose. You're like me. You'll always see more than other people do. But you need to find Polly and help her."

"Oh, what do you care anyway? You hate her. You tried to kill her twice."

"No. I didn't try to kill her. I tried to show you that she was already dead."

I stared at her. "You scared her. You scared me."

Winnie shrugged. "The two of you were getting on my nerves. Singing in my attic. Laughing. Looking at my mother's shoes. Messing around with my stuff."

"You were jealous because I had a friend and you didn't."

Winnie's eyes flashed. "So maybe I was. She was dead, like me, so why should she be happily carrying on as if she were alive? She needed to know the truth. And you needed to wake up out of your little fantasy."

I clenched my fists. "I may be like you in a lot of ways, Winnie, but I hope I'll never be as mean as you are!"

She smiled. "Ah, but you are, you know. You keep running away from all the poor ghosts who need your help. It would be so easy for you to help them, and you just turn your back."

"I didn't turn my back on you, and don't you dare say it was easy!"

"Well, maybe this is the beginning of something new for you. You helped me, you helped your father. Now help Polly, if she's such a good friend of yours."

"But—"

Winnie raised her hand to stop me. "Do what you want. I won't bother you anymore. I won't bother anyone anymore. I'm going."

And then she went. Faded away, like the Cheshire Cat, leaving me with the memory of her twisted, wicked smile.

DRIFTING

Polly

It seemed like I was drifting for a long time, floating in that white place where I couldn't see anything or hear anything. It was like that peaceful feeling when you're almost, but not quite, asleep. It wasn't scary anymore. But then I started hearing voices again, all in a jumble, like a radio flipping from station to station. I strained to make out what they were saying, and slowly they started making some kind of sense.

I could hear my mother.

"I don't know what came over me, Ned. I just completely broke down. So embarrassing. But they were very kind, and it turns out their little girl was sick last summer too, same thing as Polly. But—but—they got help in time, and she survived."

My father.

"Don't cry, Pat. Don't cry. We can't keep blaming ourselves. We'll go mad."

My brothers.

"I still say she's the Ghost Girl." (Mark)

"No, that's the other one, the dead one. I think she's nice.

They're like good twin and bad twin. Rose is like me, the good twin, and the witchy one is like you, the bad twin." (Matthew)

Some scuffling noises as they started to wrestle.

My sisters.

"Mum isn't feeling very well so I'm making supper." (Lucy)

"You can't cook." (Moo)

"Neither can you." (Goo)

"It's only soup. Just set the table." (Lucy)

And then some dishes clattering around, and supper noises.

Time flowed in and out and around me and didn't really seem to mean much. Then I heard some different voices, voices I'd never heard before.

"She needs to be around other children." (A woman.)

"Maybe she'll make some friends at school soon." (A man.)

"Do you think there's something wrong with her, Will?" (The woman again.)

"No. She is very sensitive—and certainly unusual—but I don't think there's anything really wrong with her. She needs to spend less time by herself." (The man.)

"We'll just have to get some things organized for her," said the woman firmly.

"Hmmm," said the man.

Then I heard someone singing softly. A song about a swallow.

Rose

I finished the song and waited. Nothing.

I sighed and pulled the lilac shawl closer around my shoulders. It was Sunday afternoon and I was sitting in the chair in the attic, just as I was the first day I met Polly. I thought maybe the song would bring her back.

I hummed the chorus again. It was a sad tune, but so pretty, even if the girl did die at the end. Like Polly.

Then I heard something next door. A voice.

"Rose? Is that you?"

THE GHOST IN THE ATTIC

Polly

"Yes," she said. "Polly? Wait right there, I'm coming over."

I leaned my head against the wall. I was so tired, and I still had the drifty feeling, like nothing was quite real. But I could feel my blankets were all tucked up around me, and it was good to be back in my own little nest in the attic. I could hear Rose scrambling down the passage, bumping her head and her elbows and griping about the slivers. I smiled.

She came through the door, swooping her flashlight around the attic and then finally settling it on me.

"Polly!" she said in a strange, kind of intense voice, and then she just stared at me.

"Hi, Rose!" I said. "How come you're looking at me all weird, like you've never seen me before?"

She seemed to pull herself together and came over and sat beside me.

"No reason," she muttered. "I just didn't know if you'd be here today or not."

She was clutching a pale purple shawl around her.

"What a pretty shawl!" I said. "When did you get that?"

293

"Oh, um, my great-grandmother made it for me."

"I didn't know you had a great-grandmother. When did she make it? How come I've never seen it before?"

"Never mind, Polly. We have to talk."

"Okay. Except I'm kind of sleepy today for some reason. Susie must have kept me awake last night . . ."

Rose just sat there, still and quiet.

"I saw Winnie with your dad," I said, yawning. "I guess you gave him the message, huh? When was that? I can't remember. I'm all mixed up."

"Uh . . . Friday night. Day before yesterday."

"I'm glad you told him, Rose. Now Winnie can go . . . and find her swallow." I yawned again. "But why was my mother in your house? Why was she crying?"

Rose

She didn't know. She really didn't know. A wild hope gripped my heart, and I thought I could play along with her. Like the twins. Keep her there forever, pretending she was alive, and she would never know the difference.

I gathered my courage and looked into her face for the first time. She smiled back at me, the same old Polly. But something had changed. Her eyes were clouded, like she wasn't quite awake, and her skin was pale and seemed almost transparent. She was fading. No matter what I did, I was losing her.

"Rose," she said. "What's wrong? Are you crying too? Why is everybody crying?"

I brushed my tears away and took a deep breath.

"I have to tell you something, Polly," I said. "Something difficult."

"About my mother? Is she sick or something?"

"No, not about her. About you." Polly was looking worried now. "Remember all those times you thought I was a ghost?"

"I don't think so anymore, Rose, honest. I was sort of playing, anyway. You're not still mad, are you?"

I shook my head. "No, I'm not mad. But you were on to something."

"I was?"

I took her hands in mine. They were very, very cold.

"There is a ghost in your attic. And it's not me."

She looked at me, eyes wide.

"Who is it, Rose?" she whispered.

PRETENDING

Polly

Rose looked so frightened and so sad, telling me about this other ghost. Her hands were shaking in mine.

"Don't be scared, Rose," I said. "If it's another entity I'm sure you can handle it. You were so brave with Winnie, and—"

"No, it's not another entity, Polly," she said, and then she sort of gulped like she couldn't get the next part out.

"Then who is it?" I asked, looking around the attic. "There's nobody here, just us."

"Yes," she said. "Just us. You and me. And it's not me."

I stared at her.

"What do you mean?"

She swallowed. "I'm sorry, Polly. You got sick, it was bad. It was meningitis, and I had it too. It's horrible. All kinds of kids died in the city last year. You didn't come back from the hospital."

"But I did come back. I'm here. What are you talking about? Are you trying to scare me?" I had a strange, fluttering feeling in my stomach.

She shook her head. "No, Polly, I'm not. I have to tell you. You see, you've just been hanging around, not realizing—not

realizing that you are . . . a ghost . . . and pretending—
pretending—"

"I'm not pretending!" I shouted at her, dropping her hands.
"I talk to my parents every day. I go to school. I eat chocolate
cake. I'm not a ghost! Why are you doing this?"

"Think, Polly. When was the last time you talked to your
mother?"

"Yesterday. I came home with the twins from the library,
and she told them they had to get ready for Cubs and—"

"That wasn't yesterday. That was Friday, the day before
yesterday. Did she talk to you? What did she say?"

"Well, no, she didn't say much, but—"

"Polly, you've got to understand this. You died. You weren't
ready to die, so you stayed around, but nobody can see you.
Nobody but me and the twins. Think. Has anyone else said
anything to you this week? Anything?"

The fluttering in my stomach was turning into something
heavy, like I was going to throw up, and I was getting very cold.
I tried to think. I remembered listening to people, but I couldn't
remember anyone speaking to me.

"Wait a minute. Susie spoke to me. She called me 'Olly,'
and I didn't even know she could talk."

"That's because she's just learned how to talk. Six months
ago, when you died, she was just a baby."

"But she saw me!"

"Lots of babies see ghosts, Polly. Look, your mother told us
last night. She came over because of the library book, because

she thought I stole it, and then she broke down and told us you died, and how much she missed you, and she was heartbroken. Polly, she does love you, and your dad too, and now they are so unhappy and they'd give anything to have you back."

"Really?" I said. "But I don't understand. I don't feel dead."

"Don't you?" said Rose, looking at me very intently. "Don't you, Polly?"

Rose

"I do remember . . . being sick," said Polly slowly. "It all came back to me the other day, when I was waiting for you, watching by the window. I don't know why I forgot all that. I had such a bad headache, and everything hurt, and then it was all white for a long time, and then . . ."

She had been telling me this with a strange, distracted look on her face, like she was somewhere else, but then she stopped and focused on me.

"And then I came home and everything was the same, Rose, everything was just like normal, and the twins were bugging me, and Susie was taking over my room, and I went to school and came home and did my homework, and I heard you singing in the attic, and all that stuff happened with Winnie. How could I be dead, Rose? Wouldn't I know that I was dead?"

"No," I said, taking her hand again. If anything, it was even colder now. "You weren't ready to be dead, Polly, so you stayed, and you found me, and I could see you, because I can see ghosts. And you came to me for help, like all the other ghosts do, only I didn't know you were a ghost. You fooled me as well as yourself, and I didn't know until your mother told me. And I don't want to lose you, Polly, and I don't want you to believe you're a ghost, I want you to stay and be my friend. But it's not going to happen. You have to go where you belong. You have to say good-bye and you have to go. Like Winnie. You're not meant to be here anymore."

I was crying my head off now, and Polly put her arms around me and hugged me. I could feel her heart beating against mine, but she was so cold, and she felt like she was made of brittle bones, like a bird's skeleton.

"It's okay," she said, patting me on the back. "It's okay, Rose, don't cry."

THE GIFT

Polly

Rose looked at me through her tears.

"I'm sorry, Polly," she gasped. "I'm so sorry."

"I just don't understand," I said slowly. "It seems impossible. I do feel a bit weird, like I'm getting the flu or something. And I can't remember things. But dead? How can this be dead?"

She shook her head. "I don't know, Polly. I don't understand either. You always seemed more alive than anybody to me. But it's true. I heard your mother say it, and the twins told me as well. I think . . . I think once you understand it, you'll be able to go."

"Go?" I cried. "Go? Go where? I don't want to go, Rose, I want to stay. I want to stay here with you and my family. I don't want to be dead. It's horrible, it's not fair, I can't do it, Rose, you've got to make it stop." I clutched at her shawl and she shook her head again.

"I can't make it stop, Polly. It's going to happen; it's happening already. Look at your hands."

I looked down at my hands on her shawl and they didn't look right. They were white and I could almost see through them.

"No," I cried, "I can't just fade away into nothing. I won't! I refuse!" I jumped to my feet and stumbled over to the trapdoor.

"Where are you going?" Rose called out.

"I'm going to find my mother," I said, lowering myself through the door. "She'll make it stop."

I flung myself down the ladder from the loft and burst into my room. My mother was there, getting Susie up from her nap.

"Mum!" I said. "Mum."

She didn't turn around. She just kept talking to Susie, who was standing up in her crib, hanging on to the rail.

"Olly," said Susie, looking at me and smiling. "Olly."

"Oh, Susie," sighed my mother. "Why have you suddenly started saying that? Did the twins teach you to say Polly's name?"

"Mum!" I yelled, coming up behind her and tugging on her sweater. "Mum, can't you hear me?"

She gave a little shrug, as if she had an itch on her back, and lifted Susie out of the crib. "Come on, let's change your diaper," she said and laid her on my bed.

"Oh, Mum, how many times have I told you, I hate it when you change her diaper in here. It makes my room so smelly . . ."

But she didn't hear me. She kept right on changing Susie.

I circled round to look at her.

"Mum!" I yelled. "Can't you see me?"

"Olly," said Susie.

My mother didn't even blink. She looked tired, and sadder than I'd ever seen her look.

"Polly's gone," she said to Susie. "She's gone." And then she sat down on the bed and started to cry.

I hated it when my mother cried. She hardly ever cried in front of us, but when she did it always felt as if the world was coming to an end.

I sat down beside her.

"Don't cry, Mum," I said, tears falling down my own cheeks. "I'm right here. I'm not gone yet. Don't cry."

"Polly," she said, but her eyes looked right through me. "Polly, I miss you so much."

Susie looked at us curiously. "Olly!" she said again.

"I'm scared, Mum," I said, leaning my head against her shoulder. "I'm so scared."

I sat with her for a long, long time. Gradually she stopped crying.

"My little Polly," she murmured. "My sweet girl."

"Pat?" came my father's voice from the doorway. "Pat, are you okay?"

She stood up and wiped her eyes.

"Yes, I'm fine, Ned. It just came over me, all of a sudden. It's funny, though, sometimes I feel that Polly is here, in this room."

He came in and looked around. His glance passed right over me.

"I think you're right," he said. "I'm glad we've left everything the way it was." He sighed.

"I must get on," said my mother, picking up Susie. "Lucy

said she'd take Susie for a walk, and I promised the boys I'd make some oatmeal cookies." She bustled out.

My father stepped over to the shelves and took down a book. It was *The Voyage of the Dawn Treader*, by C.S. Lewis. He used to read to me when I was younger, and that was one of our favorites. He sat down on the bed and opened it, flipping through. Then he closed it and shut his eyes.

"Polly," he said in a ragged voice I'd never heard from him before. "Polly. Where are you?"

"Here," I said, slipping my hand into his and giving it a squeeze. "I'm right here, Dad."

He just kept sitting there with his eyes shut, making no sign that he heard me. Then he made the sign of the cross across his chest. "Go in peace, Polly. Rest in peace."

Rose

I curled up under Polly's blankets in the corner by the wall. I thought she'd probably come back soon. I closed my eyes and fell asleep.

I dreamed of the ocean. Vast, blue, stretching in all directions. I was lying on a raft, bobbing gently up and down as the water rolled beneath me. The sky was a brighter blue above me, and the sun felt warm on my skin. A sense of peace stole over me, and I felt that I would be happy to go on floating like that forever, buoyed up by the deep water below me, cradled by the rocking waves, warmed by the sun.

Suddenly Polly was there beside me on the raft. She smiled at me and gave a big sigh.

"This is the life," she said, and then I woke up.

Polly was sitting beside me in the attic, her head leaning against the wall.

"Polly," I said, struggling to sit up. "Are you okay? Did you find your mother?"

She nodded. "She couldn't see me," she whispered. "Neither could Dad. You're right."

She was paler than ever.

"I'm so sorry," I said. I really didn't know what to say. I had a pain in my throat.

"I'm scared, Rose," she said in a small voice. "I don't know what's going to happen. I want my mother. But she can't see me! I don't want to go. I want everything back the way it was, the Horrors and my awful sisters and the baby taking my room and everything. I want it all back."

She clung to me.

I could barely speak. "Polly, I wish I could give you everything back, but I can't. All I know is that wherever you're going, it won't hurt anymore."

"But it hurts now," she cried. "It hurts too much."

I stroked her hair, the way the old lady had stroked mine, and I patted her back, and she cried.

Time seemed to stand still. I was aware of her frail body and her tears. I was aware of the attic walls around us, and outside, the sky going on and on. The cemetery. The world turning. I didn't want the moment to end. I willed it not to end.

But eventually she stopped crying. And then she sat up and looked at me. She smiled. It was a ghost of the old Polly smile, but it was still there.

"Don't cry, Rose," she said. "You're right. We can't do anything about it."

"If you'd never met me," I said miserably, "you'd be able to stay. You wouldn't know you were dead."

She sat forward. "But it wouldn't have been any good. I would have just got lonelier and more unhappy, thinking that nobody loved me because nobody ever talked to me. If not for you I'd have been drifting forever. Can't you see, Rose? I was meant to meet you. You were the only one who could help me get through this. Just like you were the only one who could help Winnie. You have the most wonderful gift, Rose, and you don't realize it."

It didn't feel like a gift. Right at that moment it felt like the most terrible curse. To make a friend like Polly, and then to lose her. What kind of a gift was that?

"Don't go," I said, starting to cry again. "Stay. Don't leave me."

She put her arms around me. They were light and almost weightless, like the touch of feathers.

"I'll miss you so much," I said. "You've been such a good friend to me, and I've had so much fun with you. You're— you're the best ghost I ever met."

I could feel her starting to shake. I pulled back from her embrace, and then I realized she was laughing.

"That's a really silly thing to say, Rose," she said, and then I started laughing too.

Finally we wiped our eyes and looked at each other.

"I'll never forget you, Polly," I said.

"Me neither," she replied. Her face looked translucent, and it seemed like there was a white glow spreading inside her, lighting her up from within.

"Good-bye, Rose," she said softly.

"Good-bye, Polly," I said, and watched as the light surrounded her and then faded away.

I was alone again.

TOAST

Rose

Life went on without Polly. Every day got shorter as October moved slowly towards Halloween. I wore the shawl all the time, except at school. I felt the kindness of the old lady, my great-grandmother, wrapping around me whenever I wore it.

I missed Polly more than I could say. She was the only friend I'd ever had. I wanted her back.

The things she said to me in the attic that last Sunday kept rattling around in my head. She had always behaved as if it was really cool that I could see ghosts, and I thought that was because she didn't understand how scary it was. But she was right about Winnie and my father. Winnie didn't exactly stop being scary once I helped her, but she did go away. And Polly— well, I guess I helped her to go too, although everything in me had wanted her to stay.

All this time I had thought that ghosts wanted me to make them alive again, but maybe they wanted something quite different.

At least I didn't have to worry anymore about my parents sending me away, like Winnie. I wanted to talk to my father about Polly, but I couldn't. Not yet. I was too used to not talking. And even though they said things were going to change, so far nothing much was different. I still came home from school most days to an empty house, with Kendrick lurking in the kitchen and giving me dirty looks. My parents did try talking to me at breakfast a few times, but it was all rather awkward.

One morning, just before Halloween, I was sitting draped in my purple shawl, poking at my porridge, while my parents read the paper and the Breakfast Ghost looked longingly at my toast.

"Rose," said my mother suddenly.

I jumped. "Yes?"

"Yesterday I had a little visit with Pat Lacey, next door. I dropped in after work."

"You did?" I asked, amazed.

"Yes, she asked me to. She felt so bad about the night she came over and accused you and got so upset. She wanted to apologize. She's a very nice woman, I have to say—down-to-earth, energetic. And her husband, Ned, breezed in just before I left, and he was quite charming, and he was full of apologies too, for his argument with your father when we moved in, remember? About the parking?"

I nodded.

"Well, we all started out on the wrong foot. They are a perfectly good family, and they've been through such a hard time this last year, I really feel for them. Pat and I put our heads together and we've come up with a plan."

My heart sank.

"She wants to offer you a little part-time babysitting job. She needs help with Susie around dinnertime on Tuesdays and Thursdays. Her girls are all busy with school activities those days, and it's hard for her to get the dinner made with the little boys running around and Susie demanding attention. So she thought you could come over after school, help out with Susie, and then stay on for supper with their family."

My mother looked at me as if she expected me to say something.

I didn't. I was too busy trying to sort out whether I was mad or interested.

"Well, Rose?" she said with a little twitch that meant I had had long enough to consider my answer.

"Are you just palming me off on them because you and Father still don't have time for me?"

I could see her counting to five before answering. Not ten. That would take too long.

"That's rather an unfortunate attitude, Rose," she said, finally. "I'm just being practical. Your father and I are doing our best to free up more time to be at home. But it's complicated, and it's not going to happen overnight. Meanwhile, you could do with the company of other children, and Pat really could use the help."

She had me and she knew it.

"Okay," I said with a shrug, and I ate a spoonful of porridge. The Breakfast Ghost sighed.

I broke off a piece of toast, spread it with marmalade and

pushed it over to him. My mother had gone back to her paper. But my father was watching me.

"Take it," I whispered fiercely to the ghost. "Take it, if you can."

For a moment the ghost was so startled he didn't do anything. Then he reached out carefully and brought the toast to his lips and took a big bite.

FLIGHTS OF ANGELS

Rose

I clutched the purple shawl close around my shoulders, under my cloak. It was cold, with a smell of snow in the air. It was two days after Halloween, and I was going to the cemetery to look for Polly's grave.

Mrs. Lacey had told me where to find it. I had been over to their house to help with Susie on Halloween, and, I have to admit, I'd had fun. Polly's family was exactly the way she described it: Lucy was stuck-up and snobby and used a lot of big words, Moo was drippy and Goo was caked with makeup, and everyone talked at once and the Horrors were dressed up as pirates and doing a lot of jumping around and yelling. Their noisy dinnertime seemed like a circus compared to my quiet suppers in our empty dining room. Mr. Lacey was going on about the origins of Halloween and how today was called All Soul's Day, the day to pray for the spirits of the dead.

Eventually nearly everybody had gone about their own Halloween business, and I'd put Susie to bed and looked around Polly's room at her books and her old dolls. I kept feeling that she would appear any minute, but she didn't. Her presence was everywhere in that house—and yet she was gone.

I waited till today to go to the cemetery. It seemed fitting to visit Polly's grave on All Soul's Day. I wanted to get there while it was still light, so I hurried over as soon as I got home from school, looking nervously through the iron railings for ghosts. Suddenly the stone gateposts of the cemetery loomed up ahead of me. Beyond them, the road twisted into darkness.

After walking for half a minute I left the road and headed along a path that led off to the left, past gravestones that were newer and smaller than the Victorian monuments. I had never been in this part of the cemetery.

I looked over my shoulder. The shadows were gathering behind me. I thought I caught a glimpse of something flickering through the trees, but when I focused on it, it was gone.

The path led nearly all the way to the railings that bordered Sumach Street. When I got to the end, I turned right and counted ten big steps. I stopped in front of a newish-looking granite headstone. I bent over to read the inscription in the fading light.

Pauline Margaret Lacey
March 4, 1951, to April 8, 1963
May flights of angels sing thee to thy rest.

And underneath that was the outline of a bird with a forked tail, flying, wings outstretched. A swallow.

FREEDOM

Rose

I was expecting the swallow. Mrs. Lacey had told me to look for it.

"That was Ned's idea," she'd said. "When you see a swallow, it means that spring is coming, and with spring comes new life, and hope." She smiled at me. "It's too bad you never met our Polly. I think you two would have been friends." Then she went back to yelling at the twins for eating too much Halloween candy, and I went home.

It made it so final, seeing her grave. I shivered.

Something pulled at my cloak and I whirled around.

It was the little girl who had followed me before in the cemetery when I'd first met Polly, the one with all the blond curls and the long white nightgown.

"Mama?" she said, reaching up her arms to me. "Mama?"

I felt the familiar panic and looked around wildly to see if there were any other ghosts coming. The cemetery was nearly dark now, and shadows stirred among the gravestones. I wanted to run for the gates.

"Mama?" she said again, her eyes filling with tears.

I held out my hand to her and she clutched it. Her hand was warm.

"Let's go find your mama," I said, and we walked slowly together along the lines of graves. The cemetery was full of shadows. Some were moving. Some were still. There was a whispering all around me, and I couldn't tell if it was coming from the trees moving in the wind or from deep under the ground.

We came to a tall, black tombstone with a veiled figure on top.

"Mama?" said the girl, and a woman in a long black dress with ruffles around the bottom stepped out from behind it.

"Vicky," she cried, and the child broke away from me and ran into her arms. Then they both faded away into the gathering gloom.

That wasn't too hard, I thought, taking a deep breath and turning towards the cemetery gates. The whispering died away behind me, and I walked home, along the cemetery side of the street. It was okay.

The streetlights were on now. As I got close to Polly's grave, I slowed down and peered through the railings. I could just make out the engraving of the soaring swallow, flying to freedom.

THE END

In the golden light'ning
Of the sunken sun,
O'er which clouds are bright'ning,
Thou dost float and run,
Like an unbodied joy whose race is just begun.

PERCY BYSSHE SHELLEY, "TO A SKYLARK"

In memory of Julia Poplove
1954–1991

❧

ACKNOWLEDGMENTS

I owe my love of reading and writing to my parents, Graham and Evelyn Cotter. My father introduced me to C.S. Lewis and the Narnia books when I was seven; the description of the attics in *The Magician's Nephew* captured my imagination and I have been looking for secret passages ever since. My mother held up a high standard of writing for me as I grew up, and even in her 90th year she kept her sharp eye for grammar mistakes! My parents always wholeheartedly supported my writing and I could not continue to do it without their help. My steadfast daughter Zoe kept me coming back to this book whenever I faltered, and her ghostly experiences as a child were the source of my original inspiration. And the generous funding from both

The Canada Council for the Arts and The Ontario Arts Council made this book possible.

The Swallow is about friendship, and as I wrote it I was blessed with many good friends in Newfoundland and Ontario who listened, read early drafts, offered advice, fed me and generally kept me going in tough times. Frank Lappano and Sean Cotter gave me feedback on early versions, and Wanda Nowakowska was invariably gracious and affectionate whenever I asked for help. Robin Cleland's uncanny insight into my characters helped enormously, and Anita Levin and Camilla Burgess believed in me and helped me find my way through the darker parts of the book. My "twin," Laurie Coulter, has been a cherished source of cheerleading, professional perspective and laughter.

I would like to thank Sally Keefe-Cohen for her expert advice and Lisa Moore for her encouragement when I most needed it. Special thanks to Alison Morgan for being so attentive to my stories, both during that long ago summer in Warkworth and more recently! And I owe many thanks to my editor at Tundra, Samantha Swenson, whose patience, thoughtful suggestions, enthusiasm and skill has been much appreciated. Thanks also to Kelly Louise Judd for her spooky cover and to Leah Springate for her clean design.

And finally, I send thanks to my three Graces: Julia Poplove, Marjory Noganosh and Evelyn Cotter. Their spirits have echoed through my writing in this book, and I miss them.